A Tangled Web

Carola got out of bed and pulled the curtains back slightly.

The moonlight streamed in, and she stood for a moment entranced by the beauty of the night.

It was so lovely, so part of her dreams, that she felt it could not be real.

Suddenly she heard a sound behind her.

Carola turned her head.

A man was silhouetted against the light from the corridor.

She knew who it was and was suddenly afraid . . .

A Camfield Novel of Love by Barbara Cartland

"Barbara Cartland's novels are all distinguished by their intelligence, good sense, and good nature. . . ."

— ROMANTIC TIMES

"Who could give better advice on how to keep your romance going strong than the world's most famous romance novelist, Barbara Cartland?"

— THE STAR

Camfield Place,
Hatfield
Hertfordshire,
England

Dearest Reader,

Camfield Novels of Love mark a very exciting era of my books with Jove. They have already published nearly two hundred of my titles since they became my first publisher in America, and now all my original paperback romances in the future will be published exclusively by them.

As you already know, Camfield Place in Hertfordshire is my home, which originally existed in 1275, but was rebuilt in 1867 by the grandfather of Beatrix Potter.

It was here in this lovely house, with the best view in the county, that she wrote *The Tale of Peter Rabbit*. Mr. McGregor's garden is exactly as she described it. The door in the wall that the fat little rabbit could not squeeze underneath and the goldfish pool where the white cat sat twitching its tail are still there.

I had Camfield Place blessed when I came here in 1950 and was so happy with my husband until he died, and now with my children and grandchildren, that I know the atmosphere is filled with love and we have all been very lucky.

It is easy here to write of love and I know you will enjoy the Camfield Novels of Love. Their plots are definitely exciting and the covers very romantic. They come to you, like all my books, with love.

Bless you,

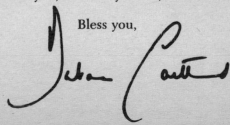

CAMFIELD NOVELS OF LOVE
by Barbara Cartland

A NEW CAMFIELD NOVEL OF LOVE BY

BARBARA CARTLAND

A Tangled Web

JOVE BOOKS, NEW YORK

A TANGLED WEB

A Jove Book / published by arrangement with
the author

PRINTING HISTORY
Jove edition / July 1991

ISBN: 0-515-10617-8

Jove Books are published by The Berkley Publishing Group,
200 Madison Avenue, New York, New York 10016.
The name "JOVE" and the "J" logo
are trademarks belonging to Jove Publications, Inc.

PRINTED IN THE UNITED STATES OF AMERICA

10 9 8 7 6 5 4 3 2 1

Author's Note

In 1860 a Belgian built what was virtually a double-acting steam engine adapted to work as a two-stroke engine with electric ignition.

At the Paris Exhibition five years later there was a free-piston engine, and in 1885 a small version of the Daimler engine was fitted to a boneshaker bicycle with two stabiliser wheels

The English went ahead with their designs for a new Daimler while the French in 1890 introduced the first Peugeot which was laboriously driven from Paris to Lyons that year.

Not to be done down, Daimler produced a year later a quite comfortable four-seater car and after that the race was on to design and produce cars which would attract the sportsmen of every nation.

The Americans were rather behind and Henry Ford produced his first experimental car in 1896.

A Tangled Web

chapter one

1896

CAROLA, riding home, passed Brox Hall.

She thought, as she had often done before, that it was the most beautiful house she had ever seen.

It was of her favourite period, having been designed in the middle of the eighteenth century.

The statues on the roof were silhouetted against the sky.

What always depressed her, however, was that the windows were mostly boarded up.

The huge house was empty except for the two old Caretakers who had been there for years.

What made it all the more sad, she thought, was that the Marquis of Broxburne was in London.

According to her brother, who knew him, he was enjoying himself.

"Why can he not come home, open the house, and spend some time on improving the estate?" she asked herself.

She knew the answer: There was not enough money!

It was the same, she thought, with so many aristocratic families.

Everything had become much more expensive.

The huge houses, which used to employ a great number of servants, were unable to carry on.

As she rode on she knew she should be thankful for the much smaller house in which her father's family had lived for generations.

The first Baronet had been created in the reign of James II.

In each subsequent generation there had been a son to succeed to the title.

Her brother Peter was now the Sixth Baronet.

He was exceedingly proud, not only of his name, but also of his estate.

It was, of course, very much smaller than that of the Marquis.

He was never at Brox Hall to be depressed by the sight of the fields unploughed and the hedges uncut.

There were two or three farming tenants.

But Carola thought that even they were somehow dispirited by never catching sight of their Landlord.

She rode on and, leaving the Broxburne Estate, arrived at their own.

It was a lonely part of the County.

Apart from Brox Hall, there was not a large number of families who were rich enough to possess much land, or, for Carola, more depressing still, rich enough to have many parties.

There were, however, some at Christmas.

The Lord Lieutenant, who should have been the

2

Marquis, gave a huge Garden-Party in the Summer.

It was the one chance, Carola thought, for all the various people who lived in that part of the world to meet one another.

She had the feeling when they said goodbye they always said, "See you next year."

That was the end of another chapter.

A mile farther on she had the first sight of Greton House.

It had been almost completely altered in the reign of Queen Anne.

Now it was difficult to remember that it had been built in an earlier period.

There were, however, a few rooms in the house that still had two-foot-thick walls, and windows with very small panes of glass.

The main rooms were high-ceilinged and spacious, and, as her father used to say jokingly:

"At least I can keep my head up!"

He had been a tall man, just as Peter was.

Carola thought it was a good thing that she took after her mother, who had been small and graceful.

But, alas, fragile, so that a year earlier she had followed her husband to the grave.

"Mama just did not want to go on living," Carola said so often.

She hoped someday she would meet somebody who would love her just as her father and mother had loved each other.

There did not seem to be much likelihood of it at the moment.

Few young men from the neighbouring families

wished to remain in the country, unless they were married.

They had gone to London like her brother.

They enjoyed themselves in the same manner in which the Prince of Wales had set the fashion.

Carola realised they had love-affairs with the professional Society Beauties whose photographs were to be seen at every Stationer's shop.

They also took the glamorous Gaiety Girls out to supper.

She remembered Peter telling her how alluring this was and how they dined at Romano's in the Strand.

To a young man, she was told, it was the most thrilling thing he could do.

"It is too expensive for me," Peter complained.

"Expensive?" Carola asked. "Do you mean the food?"

There had been a slight pause before Peter had replied quickly:

"Yes, the food and, of course, the flowers one has to send them."

He had changed the subject, but Carola found it hard to understand.

When her mother had been alive, it had been planned for Carola to go to London and be presented at Court, if not to Queen Victoria, then to the Prince of Wales and his lovely Danish wife, Princess Alexandra.

After a year of mourning, however, none of her relatives had suggested they should chaperon her.

She had, therefore, resigned herself to living in the country.

She rode the horses and waited patiently for Peter's infrequent visits.

He was very fond of her, but she knew he came home only out of duty.

There were weeks when she saw nobody except the villagers and, of course, the Vicar.

She would, she thought, have found it very lonely if it had not been for her father's large Library.

He had added to it year by year, just as his ancestors had done.

There was always something that Carola was longing to read.

She would take a book to bed with her every night and turn over the pages until she was too sleepy to read anymore.

"I suppose," she told herself now as she rode towards the house, "I could arrange to have a few parties at home."

In fact, Mrs. Newman, the Cook who had been with them for years, had suggested it.

"Now, why don't you 'ave some of your nice friends to lunch, Miss Carola?" she asked. "I'm tired of cooking a few morsels for you, an' I'll soon be forgetting me best recipes if you goes on like this!"

"It is certainly an idea, Mrs. Newman," Carola answered, "but perhaps people would find it boring coming here, unless Sir Peter was at home."

"Sir Peter's enjoyin' hisself right enough in London," Mrs. Newman said firmly, "an' it's only right you should have your slice o' th' cake."

Carola laughed.

"I will make a list of the people whom I have

not seen for a long time," Carola answered, "and perhaps we will have a luncheon party on Sunday week."

She remembered her mother had always thought Sunday was a good day to entertain.

The neighbours were not busy, either in their gardens, shopping in the nearby Market Town, or attending charitable Committees.

She found, however, that making a list was not as easy as she had thought it would be.

Most of the girls of her own age, which was nineteen, were debutantes the previous year.

Quite a number were married.

At weekends some of them would be entertaining other friends they had met in London.

Carola could quite understand that an unattached young girl would prove an encumbrance.

She was, in fact, completely unaware of her own attractions.

She did not realise that she was far too pretty for many of her friends not to be jealous of her.

Her mother had been a great Beauty, and Carola resembled her.

She had red hair, which was very unusual, being gold at the roots but interspersed with fire.

When it caught the sunshine, it made any man who looked at her draw in his breath and look again.

There was a touch of green in her eyes, not the emerald green which was associated with villain-esses, but the pale green of a clear stream.

As usual with red-headed people, she had a translucent white skin.

First because of her mother's illness, then the

long year of mourning, Carola had received few compliments.

She had no idea how unusual her looks were.

Although she was unaware of it, the last time he had been home her brother Peter told himself he must do something about her.

'There must be someone who would chaperon her if she came to London,' he thought.

Then he decided it would be a mistake to raise her hopes only to have them dashed if he could not find anybody.

He had rather tentatively asked one or two of the beautiful women with whom he dined night after night.

But their children were all in the Nursery.

They were interested in Peter because he was so good-looking.

They had, however, no wish to be told the sad story about his sister.

As she turned in through the drive gates, Carola was thinking of Peter and some of the repairs that needed doing to the house.

She did not like to give the order without consulting him.

She had the idea that he was being rather extravagant in London, which meant he might not have the money for what was required.

"I must ask him first," she told herself firmly.

At the same time, she hated not to keep up the house as it had been in her father's time.

A tile loose or a crack in a pane of glass worried him until it had been repaired.

"When I inherited the house from my father,"

her father had said, "it was perfect. I have to keep it that way for Peter."

"Of course you must, Papa," Carola said. "And I, too, am very proud of this house. It is the most attractive home anyone could have."

She knew her father was pleased with what she said.

He kissed her and replied:

"I hope, my darling, when you marry and your home is elsewhere, you will have a house that is as attractive as this one."

Carola wanted to say she wanted a home that was filled with love.

But she thought her father might think it presumptuous of her to talk of love when she was only seventeen.

Instead, they had gone hand-in-hand into the Library to unpack some new books which had just arrived from London.

Now, riding up the long drive which was bordered by an avenue of lime trees, Carola had her first glimpse of Greton House.

Then she saw that before the front-door there was a Chaise.

It was drawn by two horses.

She knew with a leap of her heart that Peter had come home.

She did not stop to wonder why he had not let her know, or even to question whether it was him or not.

She merely put her horse into a gallop.

She reached the front-door within a few minutes.

The groom, whom she recognised as looking

after Peter's horses in London, touched his forehead.

"Good evening, Jim!" she said. "I thought as soon as I came through the gate it must be Sir Peter arriving."

"Nice t'see yer again, Miss," Jim replied.

As he spoke he started to move the horses towards the stables.

Carola dismounted and a stable-boy came hurrying towards her.

He went to her horse's head and she ran up the steps without speaking.

There was no one in the hall, but the door of the Drawing-Room was open.

To her surprise, Peter was there standing at the end of the room.

It was seldom used these days.

Instead, they usually sat in the Study which had been her father's special sanctum.

It contained a great number of sporting pictures which both Peter and Carola had loved since they were children.

For a moment, however, Carola could think of nothing but that Peter was there.

She ran towards him with a little cry of delight.

"You are home! Oh, Peter, why did you not let me know you were coming?"

Her brother kissed her and replied:

"There was no time to let you know, but I am here because I need your help."

"My help?" Carola exclaimed. "What has happened? What is wrong?"

"There is nothing wrong," Peter replied. "It is

just that I need you to help me. In fact, there is nobody else who can!"

Carola looked at him in surprise before she said:

"If you have driven all the way from London, I am sure you want something to eat or drink."

"I am not hungry," Peter replied. "I stopped for luncheon on the way here, but I could do with a drink, if there is anything handy."

"I will tell Newman to get a bottle of Papa's claret from the cellar."

She flashed him a dazzling smile and left the room.

Peter watched her go.

He thought, as he had so often done before, that she was even lovelier than when he had last seen her.

"I suppose," he said to himself, "this is something I should not ask her to do, but there is no one else, and I do not think it would do her any harm."

It took Carola only a few minutes to find Newman.

He was sitting in the kitchen with his coat off, talking to his wife.

Carola knew he went there because he had so little to do.

Just like Mrs. Newman, he would like nothing better than to polish the silver for a party.

"Sir Peter is home!" she announced as she went into the kitchen.

"Sir Peter?" Newman exclaimed. "Well, that's a surprise!"

"Yes, I know," Carola answered. "He has come

all the way from London and would like a glass of claret."

Newman was putting on his tail-coat.

"I've got a bottle 'andy, Miss Carola, just in case there's an emergency like this."

Carola laughed.

"I hope you have something really delicious for dinner, Mrs. Newman," she said. "You know how Sir Peter appreciates your food."

Mrs. Newman held up her hands.

"Why he can't let us know in advance he's comin', I don't know!" she said. "There's nothing in the larder."

Carola was not listening.

She knew that Mrs. Newman would find something delicious and she wanted to get back to her brother.

She ran down the corridor, pulling off her riding-hat as she did so.

Her hair was curly, and each curl, when it was released, seemed to spring into life.

It caught the light of the sun as she came back into the Drawing-Room.

"Newman will be here with the claret in a few minutes," she said. "Now, tell me why you are home."

She sat down on the sofa.

She was looking, although she did not think about it, very unconventional.

Because it was so hot, she had ridden without a jacket and was wearing only a white muslin shirt with her riding-habit.

Now with her hair untidy she looked like a School-Girl, not like what she was—a young woman who should be enjoying her second Season in London.

As she waited, she was aware that her brother was looking at her critically, and she asked:

"Do tell me why you are here!"

Before Peter could reply, Newman came in carrying a silver salver on which stood a decanter of claret and a glass.

"Good afternoon, Newman!" Peter said. "I expect you are surprised to see me!"

" 'Tis always a pleasure t' see you, Sir Peter," Newman replied. "And ye' knows Mrs. Newman'll do her best, but she likes t' have fair warning of when you're a-comin' home."

"I know that," Peter said, "but it was important I should talk to Miss Carola, so I set off immediately after breakfast. And, if I dock the time I spent having luncheon, I think I have beaten my own record!"

"That's somethin' you always does!" Newman beamed. "At the same time, Sir Peter, you ought to be careful down them there lanes! There's been too many accidents lately."

Peter was sipping some of the excellent claret which Newman had poured out while he was talking.

The old Butler put the decanter down on a side table and went from the room.

When he had shut the door behind him, Peter said:

"Now, Carola, I am waiting to explain to you why I am here. I think you are in for a surprise!"

"There is nothing I enjoy more than surprises,"

Carola answered. "They happen all too seldom at Greton House!"

"Well, this should make up for the scarcity of them," Peter answered.

He drank a little more claret. Then he said:

"You remember my friend, the Marquis of Broxburne?"

"I was thinking of him a short time ago as I was riding past Brox Hall," Carola admitted, "and thinking what a pity it is that he never comes home."

"That is what he intends to do now," Peter said.

Carola stared at him.

"You mean ... he is going to open the house? Oh, Peter, how exciting! How ... wonderful!"

"Yes, he intends to open the house," Peter said slowly, "and it is up to you whether it stays open."

Carola's eyes seemed to fill her face.

"Up to ... me? I do not ... understand what ... you are ... telling me."

"That is just what I am going to do," Peter said.

He put down his glass.

"You knew, of course, that I was at Oxford with Broxburne, although he had not then come into the title. He was older than me and we did not really become friends until I went to London."

Carola remembered that Peter was delighted at being included in the Dinner-Parties which the Marquis of Broxburne gave at his house in Park Lane.

He had always talked about him admiringly when he came home.

"As you know," Peter went on, "Broxburne has

never been able to open the Hall, although he has wanted to do so.''

"You did not tell me that,'' Carola said. "I always imagined he was not interested in it and thought it dull to live in the country.''

"That is the reason he gave because he was too proud to admit that it was far too expensive to keep up the house and the Estate.''

Peter paused before he added:

"Unless he gave up his house in London, and the horses he keeps at Newmarket.''

Carola thought she could understand the difficulty.

At the same time, she felt it was sad that anyone who owned such an historical house should leave it empty and also let the Estate go to rack and ruin.

As if he knew what she was thinking, Peter said:

"I think Broxburne has always dreamed that one day things would come right, and now at last he has the opportunity.''

"How?'' Carola enquired.

"I think I told you that he went to America soon after Christmas,'' Peter answered.

He had not done so, but Carola did not interrupt.

"When he was there he met a man called Alton Westwood, who is going into car production in a big way. 'Automobiles,' as they call them in America.''

"Motor cars? Automobiles?'' Carola murmured.

She had seen only two motor cars in the whole of her life.

It seemed very strange to her that people should be planning to produce them in great numbers.

Of course, she had read what had been written about cars being built in England and in France.

But she could not imagine anyone she knew having one.

"To cut a long story short," Peter went on, "Alton Westwood wants his cars sold world-wide and to make sure they do so in England he is forming a Company of which Broxburne hopes to be the Chairman."

He smiled at her and then continued:

"He will then ask several of his more important titled friends to be on the Board of Directors."

"And this American thinks they will be able to sell his motor cars?" Carola remarked, trying to understand.

"Of course they will!" Peter said sharply. "And naturally the Press will write about something which is being sponsored by people like Broxburne."

"Yes, of course, I see that," Carola replied, wondering where she fitted into all this.

"Broxburne has asked me to be on the Board," Peter said proudly, "and of course I was delighted to accept!"

There was excitement in his voice as he added:

"Only yesterday he persuaded a Duke and two Peers who are very close friends of the Prince of Wales to join. They will certainly arouse Royal interest in the Company."

"It sounds very exciting," Carola agreed, "and I am absolutely delighted, Peter, that the Marquis has asked you to be on the Board."

"I would have felt hurt if I had been excluded," Peter admitted.

15

"And does it really mean," Carola asked, "that the Marquis will have so much money that he will be able to open the house?"

"Of course it does," Peter said. "Alton Westwood is already a multi-millionaire because he owns a large number of shares in an American Railway. I believe also he has found oil on his Ranch in Texas."

Carola drew in her breath.

She had heard about the enormously wealthy Americans.

It had seemed slightly unfair that England, which was a much older country, should have so many great families who were hard up.

"What Alton Westwood intends to do," her brother went on, "is to break the news to the Press about his Company and in a few months' time have an Exhibition of his motor cars in London."

"That sounds thrilling," Carola cried.

"It is," Peter agreed, "but there is a slight snag."

"What is that?" Carola questioned.

"When he was in America fixing all this up," Peter answered, "Westwood said he had heard about Brox Hall and would like to visit it. He also suggested that it would be a good idea for the Marquis to invite his friends to meet him there."

Carola stared at her brother.

"You mean bring them down ... here?"

"Yes!" Peter replied. "Westwood thinks that just to have luncheon or dinner in London is very different from spending a weekend at Brox Hall, where he can work them up into an enthusiasm about the motor car so that they can talk about it and, of course, sell the idea to their friends."

'I can see his reasoning,' Carola thought.

At the same time, she could appreciate that the American was a sharp salesman whom the English would find hard to understand.

She had read in the books that had come from London of the American style.

She thought then that the English were a little old-fashioned in their methods.

She was also aware that people like her father and mother thought it impossible for a gentleman to be "in trade."

Her mother had told her that it was the Prince of Wales who had accepted Bankers and Financiers for the first time in the history of Society.

"It will certainly be very exciting," she said aloud, "for you to see Brox Hall in all its glory."

She spoke a little wistfully, thinking it was something she would like to do herself.

"That is what you will be seeing," Peter said quietly.

She stared at him in astonishment.

"Me? What...are you...saying?"

"I am saying that when Brox Hall is open and the party they are talking about is taking place, you will be the hostess!"

There was silence before Carola said:

"I do not...believe you! Why...should the Marquis want...me?"

"That is what I am going to tell you," Peter said. "When he went to America he realised as soon as he arrived that the American women looked on him as a 'prize catch' because of his title."

"I have heard that the Americans are impressed

by titles," Carola murmured, "which is why some of our Dukes and Peers have already married American girls with huge fortunes."

Peter nodded.

"That is true and Broxburne told me that Alton Westwood was no different from the rest. He wants a title for his daughter."

"So he is married!" Carola said.

"He is married, divorced, and has a daughter a little younger than you."

"But if the Marquis marries her," Carola reasoned, "he will have that immense fortune without having to sell any of his motor cars."

"Do not be ridiculous!" Peter said sharply. "Of course Broxburne does not want to marry an American. We were talking about it the other day, and he thinks that men of our age who go posting off to America to find an heiress are bounders!"

Carola was still for a moment. Then she said:

"Of course you are right! It is wrong to marry someone either for their money, or their title."

"Exactly!" Peter agreed. "And as it happens, Broxburne has no intention of marrying anybody for years. He is in love with Lady Langley."

He saw that the name meant nothing to his sister and exclaimed:

"Surely you have heard of Lilac Langley? She is reputed to be the most beautiful woman in the whole of England, and her pictures are in every magazine as well as practically every shop-window."

"Yes . . . of course . . . now that I think about it," Carola said quickly, "I have heard of her. Is she very lovely?"

"Absolutely beautiful!" Peter replied. "And you can imagine, being in love with somebody like that, Broxburne has no intention of being caught up with some brash American girl with a heavy nasal accent."

Carola laughed.

"Is that what she is like?"

"I have not seen her," Peter admitted, "but Broxburne told me he was not attracted by any of the women he saw in New York, and he had to fight them off when he realised they were all after him."

Carola thought the Marquis sounded a rather conceited man.

As she said nothing, her brother went on:

"Then Broxburne met Alton Westwood and found that he had the same idea as everybody else."

"What do you mean by that?" Carola asked.

"Quite simply—that his daughter could be a Marchioness. Naturally, he would have preferred a Duke, but as there was not one about, he was prepared to accept a Marquis."

"The Marquis must have been somewhat surprised by that," Carola said as she smiled. "I suppose he was afraid that if he did not oblige, Mr. Westwood might not allow him to become Chairman of his Company."

"I always knew you were quick-brained!" Peter said. "And of course you are right. He was beginning to feel that it was a choice between giving in to Westwood's very broad hints, or returning to England empty-handed!"

"So what did he do?" Carola asked.

"He had a sudden inspiration," her brother replied. "He told Westwood he had a wife."

Carola laughed.

"That was very clever of him! But did not that upset the apple-cart?"

"No, apparently Westwood took it quite calmly, and there was no more pressure on Broxburne to take his 'Li'l Gal,' as Westwood called her 'up the aisle.' "

Carola laughed again.

"I hope you congratulated him on being quick-witted!"

"I did," Peter replied, "until I realised that now his 'pigeons are coming home to roost,' and he is 'up to his neck' in trouble."

Carola looked at her brother with a perplexed expression in her eyes.

"Why? What has happened?" she asked.

"What is going to happen," Peter said, "is that Alton Westwood is arriving in a week's time and, unless Broxburne plays it very cleverly, Westwood is going to find out that he is not really married!"

"I never thought of that!" Carola said. "I do see he has a problem."

"Well, I thought of a solution," Peter said, "and that is where you come in."

Carola looked at her brother.

She realised that for the first time since they had been talking, he was frowning and obviously considering his words.

She waited, and at last Peter said:

"I suggested—and Broxburne agreed—that *you* should pretend to be his wife while Westwood is here!"

Carola sat bolt upright on the sofa.

"I am to... pretend to be the... Marquis's... wife?" she repeated. "H-how can I... possibly do... that?"

"I have been thinking about it," Peter said, "and it is quite easy. Broxburne is going to say that his wife has not been well and that is why she has not been seen in London but has been in the country."

He looked at Carola to see that she was listening and went on:

"The people who are asked to Brox Hall will be as few as possible, in fact only Broxburne's special friends whom he knows he can trust with his secret."

He paused, then emphasised his next words:

"You will play hostess just for the three nights they are here and after that Westwood will, I hope, go back to America."

"And if he does... not?"

"There is no reason while he is in London that he should mention the Marquis of Broxburne's wife, and anyway, all he wants to talk about is motor cars."

"It sounds rather dangerous!" Carola said.

"It will be a damned sight more dangerous if Westwood learns that Broxburne has lied to him!" Peter replied.

"Could he not explain that he did so simply to keep the American girls from trying to marry him?"

"That might be all right if Westwood did not have a daughter," Peter said. "He was keener than anybody else to have Broxburne as his son-in-law."

"Do you really believe the Marquis's friends will not talk to him when they return to London?"

"As they will all be offered shares in the Company together with a nice fat fee for being on the Board," Peter answered, "they are not likely to do anything that will 'upset the apple-cart'—of that I can assure you!"

There was silence until Carola asked:

"S-suppose I . . . make a mess . . . of it?"

"I do not see why you should," Peter said quickly. "After all, you have seen Mama entertaining her guests in the old days and you know how to behave. I can assure you, no American is going to be critical of anything you do."

"N-no . . . I suppose not," Carola agreed, "but . . . what if the Marquis is . . . angry and . . . thinks I have let him down?"

"As he is delighted at the idea, he will be excessively grateful if you can save him from what at the moment is a threat that could destroy the whole campaign."

Because he was agitated by the thought, Peter walked backwards and forwards across the floor before he said:

"Look, Carola, I am going to make a great deal of money out of this, and I promise you it will make a difference not only to me, but also to you."

Carola did not ask how.

She merely looked at her brother as he went on:

"I know it is something I should have done before, but I just could not afford it, and that is, to provide you with a Chaperone who would present you to the Social World."

"Provide me with a Chaperone!" Carola exclaimed.

"I learnt only the other day," Peter replied, "that there are Ladies of title who are hard up and want to make a little money, who will take a *débutante* under their wing and see that she has a very exciting time."

He drew in his breath before he continued:

"It means, of course, giving a Ball, which can be very expensive, having some beautiful gowns and also the Chaperone's fee, which can run into four figures. However, now I will be able to afford it."

"It sounds wonderful!" Carola said. "I would love to go to Balls if only for a short time to see what they are like."

"Then all you have to do," Peter said, "is to pretend for three days and nights that you are the wife of the Marquis of Broxburne, who is, incidentally, a very decent chap."

He looked at her searchingly before he finished:

"I have already told you that he is in love with somebody else, so he is not likely to make a nuisance of himself."

"No . . . of course not," Carola said. "I was not thinking of that . . . I was only wondering if I . . . can do it."

"Then you agree?" Peter asked.

"Very reluctantly, dearest," Carola admitted. "But you know I want to help you, and it will be wonderful to have a little money to spend on the house. I was going to tell you there are several repairs that need to be done."

"If this deal comes off," Peter said, "we shall not only have the repairs done to the house, but new curtains, carpets, and anything you wish."

Carola gave a cry of delight.

"That is the best news I have ever heard! But, Peter, if I am to pretend I am the Marquis's wife, you will have to help me."

"Everybody will help you," Peter said, "especially the Marquis. He has more to lose than any of us."

"I expect he will want to do up the house," Carola said softly.

"Of course he does! What man would not? But do not forget, it all has to be done in a week!"

"But . . . that is impossible!"

Peter shook his head.

"Nothing is impossible if you can afford it, and because I was quite certain you would be sensible about this, Broxburne is already engaging a Firm who will fill his house with servants."

Peter paused for breath and went on:

"I have already found out the names of local tradesmen who will clean the rooms, polish the windows, and get the whole house in order before the staff arrive."

"You are taking my breath away!" Carola exclaimed.

"I have always thought of myself as an organiser," Peter said proudly, "and this, Carola, is organisation on the grand scale. And there is a big 'jackpot' at the end of it!"

Carola rose from the sofa.

"Whatever happens," she said quietly, "we must not make any mistakes."

"That would be disastrous," Peter agreed, "besides having large bills to meet which none of us, including Broxburne, can afford."

Carola looked at her brother.

"I expect by now Newman has your bath ready," she said, "so I will go to change. I feel rather as if I were in a whirlpool and it is very difficult to find my way out!"

Peter put his arm around her shoulders.

"You are a real sport, Old Girl!" he said. "I assure you, Broxburne and all the rest of us will be exceedingly grateful."

"I am already feeling as if I have a hundred butterflies fluttering inside me!" Carola said.

"All you have to do," her brother answered, "is to look pretty and say as little as possible."

"It sounds easy, but do not forget, I must have some decent gowns. I have bought nothing new since I came out of mourning, and my other clothes are too short and too tight!"

"I thought you would say that," Peter said as he laughed, "and I therefore brought a hundred pounds in cash for you to spend on clothes."

"A hundred pounds?" Carola gasped. "But that is far too much!"

"Do not forget you are a Marchioness, and West-wood will expect all the pomp and ceremony possible for a real live Peeress!"

Carola laughed.

"Oh, I forgot to tell you," Peter added. "Broxburne says he will bring with him his mother's jewellery which at the moment is in the Bank for safe-keeping. You will need a tiara and, of course, necklaces, bracelets, et cetera, galore."

Carola did not answer.

She knew from what she had read in the Social columns that a Lady of Quality always wore a tiara at dinner and on important occasions.

In fact, the Prince of Wales insisted upon it.

"Now I know," she said aloud, "that the Marquis is my 'Fairy Godfather,' and with a wave of his magic-wand I shall be correctly attired for the Ball! At the same time, do not forget that at midnight, like Cinderella, it all vanishes and I will be back in my rags!"

"There must be no 'midnight' where Westwood is concerned," her brother said firmly.

"Then keep your fingers crossed," Carola said. "Quite frankly, if I am honest, Peter, while I understand that this is something I *have* to do, I am very . . . very frightened!"

chapter two

CAROLA spent an exciting time buying three pretty evening gowns in the nearest Town.

She had decided that for the day she could wear her mother's clothes.

They had in the last two years altered very little in style.

For the evening, however, her mother's clothes would have looked old-fashioned.

She found some very pretty ones at a price which would have horrified her had it not been for the hundred pounds which Peter had given her to spend.

When she looked at herself in the mirror she thought that at least the Marquis would not be ashamed of her.

She remembered, too, that he was bringing the Broxburne jewels down from London for her to wear.

In the last week Peter had left the house very early in the morning and returned only for dinner.

The Marquis had given him the task of seeing that everything at Brox Hall would be ready in time for the visit.

He himself was staying in London in order to prepare his friends for Mr. Westwood's arrival, also to meet him when he did.

"Keep him in London for as long as you possibly can," Peter had begged.

He was not being optimistic that the Marquis would be able to do so.

It was obvious that Mr. Westwood was a very strong-minded and determined man.

He did exactly what he wanted.

From what Peter had heard of him, he was not surprised that the Marquis was afraid of finding himself married to his daughter.

He thought with a slight feeling of amusement that of the party he himself had the least important title, although it was the oldest.

He could therefore breathe freely when Westwood arrived.

The Duke was married but the two Peers were single.

Peter was not certain who else of his closest friends the Marquis intended to invite.

"Fortunately," he told Carola, "there is not as much to be done at the Hall as I had feared."

"I have always longed to go inside it," Carola said. "Is it very impressive?"

"It will certainly impress Westwood," Peter answered, "and considering it has been shut up for so long, there is really very little real damage."

Then he added:

"One or two ceilings have been stained by rain,

but they are mostly on the top floors, which we will not be using."

"I am longing to see the State Rooms," Carola said, "but, most of all, the Library."

"I grant you that is very impressive," Peter replied, "but I would be surprised if Westwood is much concerned with books."

The days seemed to fly by at a frightening speed.

When Carola came down to breakfast Peter said:

"They are arriving tomorrow!"

"Tomorrow!" she exclaimed. "But I thought the Marquis was going to keep Mr. Westwood in London."

"That is what we had hoped," Peter said, "but he is determined to hold his meetings in congenial surroundings and is apparently not particularly impressed by the Marquis's house in Park Lane."

"I imagine the houses on Fifth Avenue are larger," Carola replied, "and have more treasures in them, if what I have read is correct."

"What do you mean by that?" Peter asked.

"Well, I understand that the Vanderbilts, for instance, have collected an enormous number of antiques from all over Europe and the rooms in their New York house are stuffed with them like a pot of *pâté de foie gras*!"

Peter laughed. Then he said:

"For Heaven's sake, do not say anything like that to Westwood!"

"No, of course not," Carola replied. "Every minute I have had to spare this week I have been reading books on America until I am filled with a whole lot of information which will make it easier to talk to Mr. Westwood and his daughter."

"Be careful what you say," Peter said warningly.

"Of course, if you prefer, I will just sit looking dumb!" Carola remarked. "But I think they would find that rather dull!"

"You are deliberately upsetting me!" Peter protested.

"On the contrary, I am putting on a brave front," Carola answered, "because, as you know, I am terrified in case I do something wrong."

"I was just thinking," Peter said as if he had not been listening, "that the best thing would be for you and me to go to the Hall this afternoon."

Carola looked at him in surprise, and he said:

"I feel I know every inch of the house by this time, but it will all be new to you and it would be a mistake for you to be heard asking your way to the Library, or enquiring if the Drawing-Room is upstairs or down."

"Now you are being unkind," Carola complained. "Even so, I think it is a good idea and you can show me all over the house, which I am longing to see. Then we can be waiting on the doorstep when the party arrives."

"They are coming by train," Peter told her, "so perhaps I ought to be waiting on the platform, or, rather, at the Halt, as the Marquis has arranged one so that any train will stop there when he wishes!"

"Goodness me, how grand!" Carola said. "I never thought of them coming by train."

"The Marquis is trying to impress Westwood that America does not have a monopoly where Railways are concerned," Peter said, "and he told me when he wrote that he is trying to have his father's private coach attached to the Empress train."

"A private coach!" Carola cried. "I have always longed to see one, but I have no doubt Mr. Westwood has one himself in America."

"I am sure he has," Peter agreed. "As he owns at least one Railway, I imagine he could have a whole train for his guests, if that is what he wants!"

They both laughed at the idea.

Everything her brother said made Carola feel that the part she had to play was extremely difficult.

However, when he arrived for luncheon, Peter brought with him not only a Chaise in which he could drive her to the Hall but also a Brake for their luggage.

There was a coachman and an attendant she had never seen before in charge of the Brake.

When they drove away from Greton House, Carola asked:

"Are all the servants strangers?"

"All except for the old Caretakers who I have told to keep to their own quarters and leave everything to the new staff."

"Then no one is likely to recognise me because they have seen me in the village?"

"No one!" Peter said firmly. "They all arrived two days ago from London, and I told them that the Marchioness has been staying with friends. I said I would be driving her back today so that she will be here for her husband's return."

Carola gave a little shudder.

She did not know why, but the thought of the

Marquis being referred to as "her husband" made her feel frightened.

Peter always spoke of him either as "Broxburne" or else "the Marquis."

It was only yesterday that Carola remembered she did not even know his Christian name.

"I suppose I should know it, seeing he is a neighbour," she said, "but I cannot remember hearing it."

"It is Alexander," Peter replied, "which I think is very appropriate."

"Why?" Carola enquired.

"Because Alexander is always the name for Generals or Kings, and that, in his own way, is exactly what the Marquis is!"

"You mean he is authoritative and overwhelming?"

"Exactly!" Peter said as he smiled. "But there is no need for you to be frightened of him. Do not forget that it is *you* who are doing *him* a favour."

"Do not speak too soon, and keep your fingers crossed!" Carola said. "I might make a frightful mistake and then, if the whole plan collapses about his ears, he will blame me!"

"Now you are frightening me!" Peter said. "And for God's sake, bow to the new moon, or whatever else it is you do for Good Luck, and hope that Dame Fortune is with us."

Carola wanted to slip her hand into his.

She felt he was speaking like a little boy who is frightened his toys might be taken away from him.

But as he was driving, she put her hand on his knee and said:

"I am only teasing, Peter. I am quite certain that with your organisation and my intelligence the Marquis will get his Chairmanship of the Board and the immense remuneration that goes with it."

"That is what we are all hoping," Peter said.

As they drove up the long drive, Carola began to feel excited at seeing the inside of Brox Hall for the first time.

She vaguely remembered her father and mother going there before the old Marquis had died.

She was too young to accompany them.

Although she had often been in the Park, fed the ducks on the lake, ridden through the woods and all over the Estate, she had never entered through the front-door.

She saw the house ahead of her.

It certainly looked very different from the day she had ridden past it when Peter had come home.

The shutters had been taken from the windows.

The panes had all been cleaned until they glittered like diamonds in the sunshine.

She was aware as they drew nearer that some men were working in the gardens.

The lawns had been cut and the yew-hedges trimmed.

Peter drew up the Chaise at the front of a long flight of steps.

As he did so, two footmen wearing the Marquis's livery appeared.

A red carpet was rolled down the steps.

There was a very impressive Butler with white hair waiting to greet them at the front-door.

"Good-afternoon, Stevens!" Peter said, and turning to Carola he added: "This is Stevens, who is looking after the house. He has been a tremendous help in getting everything arranged for His Lordship's return."

Carola held out her hand.

"Sir Peter has told me how splendid you have been," she said. "I am only sorry I was not able to be here to help."

"I hopes Your Ladyship finds everything to your satisfaction," Stevens replied.

"I am sure I shall," Carola said as she smiled.

"Tea is laid in the Drawing-Room, M'Lady," Stevens said respectfully.

"Oh, thank you!" Carola replied. "It is what I have been looking forward to after my long journey."

Peter had told her on the way that she was supposed to have come some distance.

"And do not forget, Carola," he said, "that you have been ill and you have given your Lady's-maid, who has done so much for you, a well-deserved holiday, which is why a temporary maid has come down from London with the other servants."

"I shall feel very grand, having somebody to look after me," Carola smiled.

Her mother had always had a Lady's-maid.

But Carola had looked after herself from the time she was old enough to dispense with a Nanny.

Now she would have a Lady's-maid whose sole job was to look after her and press and wash her clothes.

When she and Peter were hard up she had managed with just the Newmans and had herself done a lot in the house, like the dusting.

'This will be a holiday for me,' she thought, 'at least from the household chores.'

She knew, however, she would have to be on her guard.

It would be a disaster if the servants, let alone Mr. Westwood, guessed that she was not as grand as she was pretending to be.

She walked into the Drawing-Room and found it was just as she had expected.

On a table near the fireplace there was a large silver tray on which stood a tea-pot, a kettle which had a lighted wick under it, milk and cream jugs, and a sugar-bowl.

There were hot scones in a covered silver dish.

A variety of other plates contained cucumber sandwiches, small fairy cakes, and chocolate biscuits which Carola remembered from her childhood.

There was an iced cake as well as a rich fruit cake which was decorated with almonds.

When they were alone and she was pouring out Peter's tea, she said:

"If all the meals we have over the week-end are like this, we shall certainly have grown very fat by Monday!"

"Personally, I am going to enjoy every mouthful!" Peter said, helping himself to a hot scone. "I have been working like a slave all this week. In fact, I cannot remember having to do so much since the time I left School!"

"Well, this room looks lovely!" Carola said. "And it was clever of you to remember flowers."

"Of course I remembered them," Peter said, "and also new tapers for the chandeliers."

Carola looked up at them and thought they looked very impressive.

Because she wanted to see everything, she jumped up from the tea-table and examined the china in the cabinets.

She was thrilled by a collection of snuff-boxes displayed in a glass-topped table by the window.

Peter finished his tea and said:

"Come along! I will show you the rest of the rooms and, if you are very good, the Library!"

Carola laughed.

"You know I want to see that more than any-thing else!"

"If there are a lot of books there which you want to read," Peter said, "I am sure after this the Marquis will agree to your borrowing them."

"Do you really think he might?" Carola asked eagerly.

"You should not ask the moment he arrives," Peter said, "but I think it should be part-payment for what you are doing to make a success of the party."

"Now I know why you are holding out the Library like a carrot before a donkey!" Carola said. "But do not forget, Peter, that if I am too nervous to ask the Marquis for the loan of his books, you will have to do it for me."

"All right," Peter agreed, "but come along or we shall still be walking round the house at mid-night!"

There was certainly a lot to see.

By the time Carola had been thrilled by the

36

Music-Room and almost forcibly dragged by Peter from the Library, the sun was sinking.

Peter opened the door of the Picture Gallery.

It was very large and each picture, Carola thought, was a joy she had not expected.

"I had no idea the Marquis had such a wonderful collection!" she exclaimed.

"They are all very valuable," Peter answered, "but of course they are entailed, so there is no question of him selling any of them."

Carola turned to look at her brother.

"I had forgotten there would be an entail," she said, "and of course that means the Marquis will have to get married and produce a son."

"That is something he has no wish to do at the moment," Peter said. "He is only twenty-nine, and there is no reason for him to marry for at least ten years!"

They continued their tour of the house.

It was almost time to change for dinner by the time they reached the Nurseries.

Carola thought it sad that they were empty.

They were set out in very much the same manner as those at home, except that they were larger.

She was delighted with a huge rocking-horse and a big fort.

Even Peter was intrigued by an array of tin soldiers which seemed to include every Regiment in the British Army.

There was a large Teddy Bear propped up in an armchair.

There were a number of other toys similar to those which she and Peter had played with when they were children.

Carola picked up a Golliwog and said:

"I was just thinking—if the Marquis is supposed to be married—what will Mr. Westwood think of his not having any children?"

"I had not thought of that," Peter said. "I suppose we must attribute it to the fact that his wife has not been in very good health."

"Of course, it would be the woman who would get the blame!" Carola objected. "I must remember to look pale and of course go to bed early."

"I think that would be a good idea anyway," Peter said. "Westwood might think it was impolite to discuss business in front of you."

"Very well," Carola said, "but I hope there will be some interesting books upstairs."

When she went to her bedroom to change for dinner she found it was extremely beautiful with a huge four-poster bed.

The posts were carved and gilded.

On the canopy there was a delightful carving of Cupids carrying garlands of flowers.

"It looks very romantic!" Carola exclaimed.

"And so it should!" Peter said. "This is the Marchioness's room, and there is a communicating door which leads into the Marquis's."

"Then . . . I am . . . next . . . to him!"

"Of course you are!" Peter said. "Do not forget you are supposed to be married to him, so be careful what you say in front of your Lady's-maid."

As if he had just thought of it, he said:

"I did not tell you that the only servant who knows the truth is the Marquis's Valet. He went with him to America and knows exactly why he had to say he was a married man, so he is 'in' on the secret."

Carola thought that was a little embarrassing, but she did not say so.

Peter walked to the end of the room to open the communicating door.

"Come to see the Master Bedroom," he said. "I think it is the most magnificent room I have ever seen, and I only wish I could have one like it!"

Carola followed him, and when she saw the Marquis's room, she understood.

She was sure that any man who slept in it would feel like a King.

It, too, was dominated by a four-poster bed, but the posts, wood carved, were of oak.

The bed itself was covered in crimson velvet with the Broxburne coat of arms behind the head-board.

The curtains were of the same velvet and the walls were also panelled in oak.

There was a magnificent marble fireplace which Peter said had been brought from Italy.

The furniture had been chosen at the same time as the house had been built.

"I am not surprised the Marquis thinks he is 'Monarch of all he surveys!'" Carola remarked. "And, come to think of it, he has been a long time in surveying it!"

"Do not say that to him," Peter implored. "He is very touchy about not having been able to come here before."

Carola thought privately that, if the Marquis had economised on his amusements in London and his race-horses at Newmarket, he could doubtless have opened the Hall before now.

She knew it would upset Peter to say so, and she merely moved back into the other bedroom.

As Peter joined her she said:

"I suppose I can lock this door at night?"

"No, of course not!" Peter replied. "The servants would think it very strange. Remember— no one must have the slightest suspicion that you are not what you are supposed to be!"

He thought for a moment, then he said:

"Another thing I forgot to mention is that Westwood is bringing his own man-servant with him."

Carola looked surprised.

"I thought American men were so self-sufficient that they did not need Valets!"

"This man is not exactly a Valet, I understand, more a Secretary," Peter said, "and the Marquis said he would not be surprised if he was a spy."

"A spy?" Carola exclaimed.

"Well, you know what confidential servants are like," Peter said, "and he obviously keeps his eyes open to see that his master is not gulled too outrageously, or deceived by his so-called friends."

"I know exactly what you mean!" Carola said. "At the same time, it is frightening to know there is somebody watching me and, of course, everything you and your friends do."

Peter did not answer because at that moment the door of Carola's bedroom opened and a maid came in.

Too late, both brother and sister realised that if Carola was the Marchioness, as she was supposed to be, she would not be entertaining a man in her bedroom.

Peter quickly summed up the situation and said to the maid:

"You must be Jones, who is looking after Her Ladyship?"

The maid dropped him a curtsy.

"That's right, Sir."

"I was just showing Her Ladyship what improvements have been made to His Lordship's bedroom while she has been away."

He paused before he went on:

"Now it is time to dress for dinner, and I am sure you will look after her very well."

"I'll do me best, Sir," the maid replied.

Peter moved towards the door.

"I will see you downstairs," he said to Carola.

"I will try not to be late," Carola replied, "and thank you. Thank you very much for looking after me."

As Peter shut the door she said to the maid:

"I see you have unpacked for me, and now I would like, if it is possible, to rest before dinner."

"Yes, o'course, M'Lady," the maid said, starting to turn back the lace and satin cover on the bed.

"I expect you have been told," Carola went on, "that I have unfortunately been ill for some time and my Lady's-maid was so wonderful to me while I could do nothing for myself that I have sent her off on a holiday."

"That's very kind of Your Ladyship!" Jones said.

"I am feeling very much better now," Carola went on, "and I am sure you will not find maiding me too arduous."

" 'Course I won't, M'Lady," Jones replied.

She was a pleasant-faced woman of about forty,

and Carola was sure, well up in her duties.

As she unbuttoned Carola's gown at the back, she said:

"This is a beautiful house, M'Lady. You must be very happy living here."

"I love being in the country," Carola replied, "but it can be very cold here in the Winter."

"I 'spect that's why Your Ladyship got ill," Jones remarked.

"I am better now," Carola answered, "and I do not want to think about it anymore. I only hope it will not happen again."

"You'll just have to take care of yourself, M'Lady, and not do too much," Jones admonished Carola.

She sounded so much like her old Nanny that Carola nearly laughed.

Then, as she got into bed, she said:

"Give me plenty of time to get dressed, Jones. I do not want to be late for Sir Peter or upset the Chef."

"I'll bring in your bath at seven-thirty, M'Lady," Jones said.

She left the room and Carola laughed a little to herself.

It was such fun having a maid who would see to her bath with plenty of stalwart young footmen to carry the water upstairs.

At home they had been reduced to just the Newmans.

It had then been Peter's idea to construct a room for the bath on the Ground Floor.

It had at one time been a rather spacious Cloak-Room.

They had placed the bath in the centre of it.

Then it meant carrying the water only a short distance from the kitchen.

Here in Brox Hall, without any difficulty, the water would be brought up the stairs and along the corridor to her bedroom.

She was quite certain there would be two house-maids to pour the water into the bath.

Jones would supervise the whole operation.

"I shall have three days of sheer luxury," Carola told herself, "and I am determined to enjoy every minute of it!"

* * *

Dinner was certainly delicious.

Carola and Peter talked very discreetly while the servants were in the room.

They were waited on by the Butler and two foot-men.

There were two in the hall and another two on duty in case they were wanted.

When they were alone Carola said:

"The meal was delicious! I am hoping you are going to make a great deal of money, because for the short time we are here I will develop a taste for real luxury!"

"I was thinking the same thing!" Peter said. "I suppose you realise we have already made one mistake for which I, at any rate, should be severely reprimanded."

"A mistake!" Carola asked in horror.

"The Marchioness of Broxburne is staying here

alone with a handsome young man called Sir Peter
Greton!"

Carola looked at her brother for a moment before she said:

"I never thought of that! Of course it was a great mistake!"

"Luckily I have managed to rectify it," Peter said with a laugh.

"H-how have ... you done ... that?"

"I told the Butler, when he was asking me if everything was in order, that you were my first cousin and we were brought up together."

Carola clasped her hands.

"Oh, Peter, that was clever of you! It never entered my head for a moment that the servants would be surprised that we were staying alone here."

"I ought to have thought of it this morning," Peter said. "I blame myself entirely."

"Well, there is no harm done to the Gretons or the Marquis," Carola said.

"I hope not," Peter remarked, "but Stevens had a knowing look in his eyes which I disliked!"

"You mean ... he thought ... ?" Carola began.

"Of course he did! And it was extremely stupid of me not to have thought of it myself."

Carola did not reply, and after a moment Peter said:

"Now, look here, Carola, because you are so pretty, you have to be very careful this week-end not to become involved with any of the party."

"What do ... you mean ... by that?" Carola asked a little nervously.

She thought her brother was feeling for words before he said:

"I expect you have heard that the Prince of Wales has been infatuated with a number of beautiful women in the last few years, despite the fact that he is married to Princess Alexandra."

"I remember Mama being shocked because somebody talked about him having an *affaire de coeur* with Mrs. Lily Langtry, and she said it must be untrue."

Peter was frowning, and after a moment she asked:

"Is it true?"

"I have no idea," Peter replied quickly, "but the fact that they were talked about was a mistake, and Lily Langtry, who became an actress, was not the only one."

"Papa said something about the Prince of Wales being in love with Lady Warwick. I have seen pictures of her in the magazines and I thought she was very beautiful!"

"I am not concerned with the Prince of Wales," Peter said, "but when a beautiful woman is married, it is more or less accepted that the men who meet her pay her compliments and what you might call 'flirt' with her."

"Are you saying...they will...do that to... me?" Carola asked.

Peter thought that as his sister was so pretty, it would surprise him if they did anything else.

So as not to frighten her he said:

"Of course, those who are here will be aware that you are not actually married to the Marquis, so they may treat you as if you are a young and

45

innocent girl. At the same time, if you were married, you might find that insulting!"

Carola held up her hands.

"It is becoming more and more...complicated!" she complained.

"What you have to do," Peter said as if he had just thought of it, "is to take any compliments you receive calmly and realise that it is all part of the act and does not mean anything else."

"No, of course not," Carola agreed. "I do understand that as a married woman, if no one said anything flattering to me, I should feel I was hideous and a bore."

"I am quite sure nobody is going to think that!" Peter said loyally. "At the same time, if things seem too uncomfortable, you can always go to bed."

Carola laughed.

"I can hardly slip away to bed if I receive compliments at luncheontime!"

Peter was silent.

It was impossible to explain to his sister what he feared.

In fact, it was difficult to put into words even to himself.

The Marquis and his friends were all gentlemen.

However, because Carola was so lovely, and because she was playing a part which they all knew about, he was frightened, not because of them, but in case Carola in her nervousness should betray the whole plot.

He was sure he was making a "mountain out of a molehill."

At the same time, the danger was there.

He was sure before the week-end was over there would have been a great many difficulties and pit-falls he had not accounted for.

He realised now that Carola was looking at him.

There was a worried expression in her large green eyes.

"It is all right," he said soothingly, "and as they say in the theatres, 'It will be all right on the night!' If anything upsets you, just come and tell me."

"Of course I will do that," Carola said, "and after all, now that I am here in the house I have always longed to see, I find it very exciting and a thrilling experience I shall never have again."

That, Peter thought to himself, was exactly what worried him.

chapter three

WHEN she woke up the next morning Carola felt agitated.

This was the day—this was the frightening moment when she was to meet the Marquis for the first time.

Apart from him, she was nervous of his friends despite the fact that Peter was certain they would not talk.

She could imagine nothing more humiliating than if it was known that she was pretending to be the Marquis's wife.

He would then lose out to Westwood.

She was sure that the American would not only resent having been lied to, he would also think the nobility who were concerned in the plot were laughing at him.

"Please God," she prayed, "do not let me make a mistake...please...please!"

Peter was busy the following morning putting

the finishing touches to everything he had organised.

Carola had her breakfast in her bedroom because she thought it was easier.

When she came down she was very impressed.

Flowers were everywhere, which made the house look lovely.

They also hid any dilapidations, such as threadbare carpets or faded curtains.

She was wearing one of her mother's prettiest gowns.

She thought it would give her confidence.

It was then she remembered she should have a wedding-ring.

Fortunately her mother's was in her jewel box.

She slipped it onto the third finger of her left hand.

She felt sure her mother was helping her and preventing her from making any mistakes.

Even if Alton Westwood did not notice her, she knew the Marquis and the other guests would.

If they were not impressed, they might in some way hurt Peter.

She was glad he had such important friends.

Her mother had been worried when finally he went to London.

She was afraid he might be caught up with the raffish young men who haunted the Gaiety Theatre.

Carola guessed that they were not accepted by the more discriminating Hostesses.

However, from what Peter had told her, he had been asked to all the best houses.

He had once even been included in a party at Marlborough House.

'It is wonderful for him,' she told herself, 'and if I have to skimp and economise, I know it is what Mama would want me to do.'

Downstairs she looked into all the different rooms and inevitably ended up in the Library.

Even to look at the books was a joy she could hardly express.

If she could read even one, it would be an adventure into the unknown.

Her father had always told her she was clever.

She knew he was proud of the way she could debate with him on so many subjects.

She also had a good knowledge of the different customs to be found in other countries.

Once he had said to her:

"You ought to have been a boy, my darling."

She knew it was the highest compliment he could pay her.

'What I have to do,' she decided, 'is to use my brains and sound, when I am talking, much older than I really am.'

She had arranged her hair very carefully in an exact copy of her mother's.

Her elegant gown with its high boned collar was different from what she would have worn as a young girl.

She looked at herself in one of the gilt-framed mirrors.

She hoped that the Marquis would think she looked like the sort of woman he might have married.

She thought it was unfortunate, because her hair was so red and her eyes green.

The former Marchionesses of Broxburne would have been more prosaic and not so spectacular.

Then she turned from the mirror defensively.

"I am doing my best," she said aloud, "and if they want someone different, they should not have asked me to play the part!"

She and Peter had an excellent luncheon in the Dining-Room.

It was large enough to hold forty guests without being overcrowded.

He had decided that as they were supposed to be close cousins who had grown up together, they could call each other by their Christian names.

"You know, of course," Peter said, "that it is correct in English Society for everyone to be addressed by their full title. In fact, if you had not been obliged to call the Marquis 'Alexander,' you would address him as 'Marquis,' just as you will address the Duke and, of course, the other two Peers."

"What are their names?" Carola asked. "I should have asked you before, because obviously my 'husband' would have enlightened me as to who was coming to stay."

Peter groaned.

"Oh, Lord, not another mistake!" he murmured.

However, he gave Carola the names of the Duke of Cumbria, Lord Durrcl, and the Earl of Heverham.

Carola hoped she would be able to remember them.

At three o'clock, when they should have been arriving, Peter was more on edge than his sister.

"I only hope I have thought of everything!" he said several times.

"Of course you have," Carola said soothingly. "You have been wonderful, and no one else could have cleaned up the house so quickly!"

"It has cost a fortune!" Peter remarked. "And if anything goes wrong, Broxburne will be horrified at the bill!"

"Nothing is going to go wrong," Carola protested.

She crossed her fingers as she spoke, hoping that Peter would not notice.

They went into the Drawing-Room and she seated herself elegantly on one of the gold-framed sofas.

The satin damask with which it was covered was slightly faded, but it was in fact a perfect background for her hair and her eyes.

"There is one thing I must tell you..." Peter began.

Before he could finish the sentence, the door opened and Stevens came in to say:

"The carriages are just coming up the drive, Sir Peter!"

Without answering him, Peter moved quickly across the room and disappeared into the hall.

Carola knew he would receive the Marquis on the steps.

If possible, he would assure him that everything was in order before he entered the house.

She waited, saying a last-minute prayer that everything would go smoothly.

There was the sound of people in the hall. Some-one laughed, as if at a good joke.

Then a man came hurrying into the Drawing-Room.

Carola rose to her feet.

She realised without being told that this was the Marquis, to whom she was supposed to be married.

He was not in the least what she had expected.

Somehow from Peter's description she was expecting him to look much older, cold, hard, frightening, and autocratic.

Instead, he was young, exceedingly good-looking, and had an amused expression on his face.

He crossed the room, took her hand in his, and said in a low voice:

"Thank you a million times for helping me. You look marvellous—absolutely marvellous!"

Carola drew in her breath.

It was not in any way how she had expected to be greeted.

Then, as several more men came into the room followed by Peter, the Marquis turned round to say:

"Let me introduce you to my wife who, I am delighted to say, is well enough to be your host-ess."

"That is excellent news!" a tall man replied.

He walked towards Carola and held out his hand, and the Marquis said:

"This, my dear, is the Duke of Cumbria who is, as you know, an old friend."

"Yes, of course," Carola said, "and it is delightful to meet you, Duke! Alexander has told me so much about you."

"And I have been longing to meet you," the Duke said gallantly.

The Marquis turned and looked at the next man proceeding down the room.

Before he spoke, Carola knew it was Alton Westwood.

He, again, was not half as American-looking as she had expected.

He was tall and in fact very good-looking, with a square chin.

She was sure he was from Texas.

"Now, this," the Marquis was saying, "is the man I wrote to you about—Alton Westwood—one of the cleverest men in America. We are all delighted to be associated with him."

Carola put out her hand, and he gripped it with a strength she had not expected.

As she looked at him she saw that his eyes were very blue.

"Let me welcome you, Mr. Westwood to Brox Hall," she said. "My husband has told me how kind you were to him in America."

"And now your husband's being kind to me," Alton Westwood replied, "in bringing me here to this very fine mansion and letting me meet with you."

Carola smiled.

Alton Westwood had only a slight American accent, and she thought he certainly had a charm she had not expected.

"Now I am looking forward to introducing you to my L'il Gal!" Alton Westwood said.

He looked around him, then exclaimed:

"Where is she?"

One of the other men replied:

"Need you ask? She is patting the horses and appreciating them, as we all were on our way from the Station."

Alton Westwood laughed.

"I might have guessed that's what Mary-Lee would be doing! There's only one thing that holds my daughter's interest, and it is not automobiles, but horses!"

The other men laughed at that.

The Marquis introduced Carola to the Earl of Heverham and Lord Durrel.

Peter had disappeared, and Carola guessed he had gone back to fetch Miss Westwood.

Then Stevens and two footmen came hurrying in.

One was carrying a tray on which there were two open bottles of champagne in a gold ice-cooler and a number of glasses.

"This is what we all need after the train journey," the Marquis said, "and of course we are also celebrating, Westwood, your first visit to Brox Hall."

"Which I truly hope will not be my last!" Alton Westwood said.

Carola accepted a glass of champagne, hoping that her hand was not trembling as she held it.

The other guests were, she was aware, looking round the room and appreciating what they saw.

They were obviously hoping it would impress Alton Westwood.

It was the Duke who came up to her to say

quietly so that no one else could hear:

"I had no idea that you would be so lovely! I am drinking a special toast to your eyes."

Carola hoped she was not blushing.

She tried to reply calmly, as if it were the sort of compliment she heard every day:

"How kind, Duke, but I have been worrying more about making the house look beautiful for my husband's guests rather than myself."

She smiled as if she knew he was really appreciating her efforts to appear at ease.

He is rather sweet, she thought.

He was obviously older than the Marquis and the other men.

She guessed that he was, in fact, nearing forty.

She knew it must be a feather in the Marquis's cap to have got him to patronise Alton Westwood's venture.

She thought that, when she had an opportunity, she would thank him.

Peter came back into the room.

He was escorting a young girl whom Carola saw at a glance was very pretty.

She had somehow expected her to be muscular-looking, but instead she was delicately made with very large eyes.

She looked American, because like her father she, too, had a square chin.

She had exquisitely small feet which Carola had always been told was characteristic of American women.

Also, she had a smile that illuminated her face.

"How d'you do, Ma'am!" she said to Carola. "Sorry I got held up coming to meet you, but I was so thrilled with the horses that brought us from the Station!"

"I am delighted you should appreciate them," Carola said, "and if you want to ride while you are staying here, there are some horses in our stable which I know would be very proud to carry you."

"That's what I hoped," Mary-Lee exclaimed, clapping her hands.

She turned to her father.

"Did you hear that, Poppa? I can ride while I am here, and you know I am feeling stiff after doing nothing on board ship except play Skittles!"

The men laughed at this, and the Earl said:

"I cannot believe there were not some handsome young gentlemen for you to dance with in the evenings!"

"Oh, that!" Mary-Lee exclaimed. "Of course we danced, but it not the same as riding!"

"I can show you where the best jumps are," Peter offered, "and I cannot believe you will not fly over them on wings."

Mary-Lee laughed at this.

Then all the men were teasing her about her passion for riding.

"I would rather ride than anything else in the world!" she said firmly. "And I am prepared to challenge any English girl you care to produce!"

Peter looked at Carola.

"I am afraid this is a somewhat masculine party," he said, "but my cousin, the Marchioness, is an outstanding rider, so there is a challenge for both of you, and, of course, our host is expected to provide the prize!"

For one moment Carola thought that her riding-habit would not be smart enough.

Then she told herself that at least she would be able to enjoy riding.

And while she was doing so, she would not have to wonder whether she was doing the right thing or not.

To Mary-Lee she said:

"We will certainly show these gentlemen what we can do, and it will at least take their minds off business for a short while!"

Mary-Lee laughed.

"You are quite right, Ma'am, but you have to be up early in the morning to prevent Poppa from talking of anything else. As I often say to him—anyone who prefers automobiles to horses must be loose in the head!"

They all laughed at this, and Alton Westwood said bitterly:

"'Out of the mouths of babes and sucklings . . .' but what can I do about it?"

"She may ride her horses now," the Duke remarked, "but when your cars arrive, she must be kind enough to be photographed with them, which will mean that anyone who looks at your lovely daughter will buy a car!"

"That is a good idea, Poppa!" Mary-Lee approved. "I do not mind being photographed beside a car, as long as I do not have to drive it!"

She was obviously not in the least shy.

At the same time, she looked so very pretty when she was talking, smiling, and laughing.

Carola found herself wondering if the Marquis

was not being short-sighted in not thinking of marrying her.

She could understand that Mary-Lee was very young.

At the same time, he could not marry the beautiful Lilac Langley.

It seemed a pity to miss having Alton Westwood with all his millions as a father-in-law.

Then she told herself that although it was unlikely, perhaps the Marquis was an idealist.

He might want to marry for love.

From all she had learned from Peter, it was something that seldom happened in the Social World.

Her mother had told her that among the aristocrats, just like Royalty, marriages were arranged as soon as a girl was grown up.

Then the important thing, she had said, was to gain the highest title possible.

Carola had always felt it was very cold-blooded and it was the girl who suffered rather than the man.

She knew that any man like the Marquis had to marry sooner or later to obtain an heir.

It was to their advantage to marry into a family that in breeding was the equal of their own.

She looked at the Marquis again. He was talking animatedly to Alton Westwood.

She thought that although Peter found him overwhelming and autocratic, he also had charm.

Then she looked at his grey eyes.

She knew then he could be very determined and, if the occasion arose, forceful.

'He is determined to bring about this coup!' she

thought. 'And if he fails to do so, he will be very angry!'

She felt a little shiver go through her.

As if he realised she was nervous, Peter came to her side.

"I thought you would like to show Miss Westwood and her father the house while the servants are unpacking," he said.

"Yes, of course," Carola agreed, "what a good idea!"

She put down the glass from which she had taken only a sip and walked to Alton Westwood's side.

"I was wondering," she said, "if you and your daughter would like to see a little of the house. We shall have tea shortly, but I would love to show you the Picture Gallery if you are interested."

"I'm interested in anything that is real England!" Mr. Westwood replied. "And I'd be very honoured if you would show us this fine building yourself."

"Then that is what I will do," Carola said.

Westwood called to his daughter.

As they moved out of the Drawing-Room, Carola saw with relief that Peter was coming too.

She had not liked to ask him to do so in front of the others, but she felt it was essential for him to describe the things she had seen for the first time yesterday.

They moved from the Drawing-Room into the Library.

As Carola expected, Westwood was not particularly interested in books.

Because she felt she could not bear them to be

disparaged, she went quickly to the Music-Room.

There, to her surprise, Mary-Lee exclaimed with delight at the large Steinway piano and, sitting down at it, played a few chords.

"You did not tell me you were a pianist!" Peter said.

"Of course I can play," Mary-Lee replied.

She played the opening bars of a Strauss Waltz and, looking up at Peter, said:

"I hope I am going to have a chance to dance tonight. After all, I will have plenty of partners!"

As she spoke, Carola knew this was something Peter had not thought of, and she said quickly:

"It is very remiss of me, Miss Westwood, but I had not thought of that until now, but I am sure I can play the piano well enough for you to dance, and that is exactly what we will do after dinner."

She looked at Peter as she spoke and knew that he understood.

It would be a relief, she thought, from having to continue conversation with Mr. Westwood, which Peter had anticipated might present difficulties.

Or, for that matter, with the other members of the party.

"My cousin is right," Peter said aloud. "We can dance in here, and if the others would rather talk to your father, then we will have the floor to ourselves."

"We will want to join in all right," Westwood said, "and I for one will want to partner the Marchioness, so Mary-Lee must take her turn at the piano."

"Of course I will!" Mary-Lee agreed. "And the

Marchioness and I will be completely fair about it!"

They went from the Music-Room to the Picture Gallery, and again Carola thought that Mr. Westwood was rather bored.

Mary-Lee, however, enthused over a number of the pictures before asking if she could see some of the State Rooms.

Feeling a little embarrassed, Carola took them into her bedroom.

"All the previous Marchionesses have slept here," she said, "ever since the house was built."

She glanced at Peter as she spoke, and he explained how important the Adam brothers had been in the 1750s and how the designs for each room had never been altered.

He then took them through the communicating door into the Marquis's bedroom, and Carola knew that now Mr. Westwood was really impressed.

"Now, that's what I call a right Royal room!" he exclaimed.

"Oh, Poppa, you have got to have one just like it!" Mary-Lee insisted.

"And have all my friends pulling my leg?" Westwood asked. "No, thanks, honey, no heavy curtains and carvings for me!"

Mary-Lee pouted.

"Well, I think they are very pretty, and I want something just like this when I get married."

"You will have to find a husband with the right coat of arms to hang behind your head!" her father said.

Mary-Lee studied the Marquis's elaborate one.

"Now I see what you are after, Poppa," she said, "and it is certainly an idea!"

Carola knew that Peter's eyes were twinkling, and it was with difficulty that she did not laugh.

Instead, she took the Westwoods downstairs to where tea was waiting for them in the Drawing-Room.

It was a large, typically English tea, and she knew that both the Americans enjoyed it.

When they had finished, having eaten quite a number of cakes and nearly all the sandwiches, Mary-Lee asked:

"Now can I go look at the horses?"

Carola was a little surprised.

She would have thought that the horses, which were clearly the main attraction, could keep until tomorrow.

Before she could speak, however, the Marquis replied:

"Of course you may, but I suggest Sir Peter take you, as he knows them as well as I do, and you must forgive me as I have some letters to write before dinner."

"I would rather like a word with you, Marquis," Westwood said.

"Of course!" the Marquis replied. "Let us go into the Study."

They walked away together, and Carola thought it would be rather tiring to go to the stables.

She had been on her feet since first thing this morning.

The shoes she was wearing were her mother's and a little tight.

They were much smarter than her own and

toned in well with her gown, which was why she had put them on.

Mary-Lee, however, was determined not to miss the horses, and Peter therefore went with her to the stables.

Lord Durrel said he wanted to read the newspapers and went to the Library, where Peter had them laid out on a stool.

Carola was left alone with the Duke.

She was about to say that she would like to go upstairs and rest, when he moved to sit beside her on the sofa.

"I want to tell you," he said, "that I thought how marvellous you are, and how splendidly you have carried off everything until now."

"Do not speak too soon!" Carola warned. "I am terribly nervous of doing something wrong."

"I think that would be impossible!" the Duke said.

She realised his words were a compliment, but also the way he looked at her made her feel shy.

"I was just thinking," she said, "that I should go upstairs now and lie down before dinner."

"And leave one of your guests unattended?" the Duke complained. "That would be a very unkind thing to do."

Carola smiled.

"I think Your Grace is quite capable of looking after yourself," she said, "and I am wondering what Mr. Westwood is saying to the Marquis."

"Well, one thing is certain—he is not forcing his daughter onto him!" the Duke replied.

"She is a very sweet girl," Carola remarked.

"And very much prettier than I expected," the

Duke replied. "At the same time, Alexander, as I expect you know, is determined not to marry until he is very much older."

"I can understand that," Carola said, "and it must be very difficult for a man, if he wants to marry for love, not to be trapped when he is least expecting it!"

"That is the position in a nut-shell!" the Duke said. "And what I am suffering from myself at the moment."

Carola looked at him in surprise.

She had not thought that as a widower he would be as vulnerable as the Marquis.

Now she realised that as a Duke, he was, of course, an even better catch.

As if the Duke read her thoughts, he said:

"Exactly! And I have made it very clear to our American friend that I am still desolate after losing my wife and could never consider putting anybody else in her place."

Carola put her hand up to her forehead.

"Oh, dear," she said, "I can see you are having the same trouble as the Marquis which, I admit, I never expected."

"I have, in fact, been a widower for many years," the Duke said, "but if by any chance Westwood should ask you—I have shortened the time considerably!"

"Do not tell me . . . please, do not tell me any more things I have to remember," she said. "I am praying I will not make any mistakes, but it is very difficult."

"As I have already told you, your performance

is perfect!" the Duke said. "But I admit you took me by surprise!"

Carola looked at him enquiringly.

"I cannot imagine why I have never met you before," the Duke explained. "You are very, very beautiful—so beautiful, in fact, that you put most of the Professional Beauties in the shade!"

Carola laughed.

"Now you are teasing me, and you know the truth—I am just a country girl who knows nothing of London. I have been forced into this absurd charade so that I can help my brother."

"You are helping us all!" the Duke said. "And I for one am very, very grateful!"

There was a sincerity in his voice that was unmistakable.

Because of the way he was looking at her, Carola knew she was blushing.

Then she remembered this was the sort of conversation about which Peter had warned her.

"I think," she said, "I should go upstairs."

She would have risen, but the Duke put out his hand to prevent her from doing so.

"I want to talk to you," he said, "and I shall think it very cruel if you walk away and leave me alone."

"What do you want to talk about?" Carola asked.

"You know the answer to that—you, of course!"

"From now on this is a forbidden subject," Carola objected quickly. "It would be dangerous, very dangerous for us to talk indiscreetly."

She paused a moment and then continued:

"In any case, I have been told that if you want to have a successful disguise, you have to *think* yourself into the part from first thing in the morning until last thing at night."

"If you are insinuating," the Duke said, "that I should think of you as Alexander's wife, I intend to do nothing of the sort! I know Alexander very well and where his interests lie at the moment."

He stopped speaking for a moment to smile at her before he went on:

"I know I am not 'poaching on his preserves' by telling you that you intrigue me and I want to know a great deal more about you than I do at the moment."

Carola gave a little laugh.

"Why are you laughing?" the Duke asked.

"Because this is exactly the sort of conversation my brother Peter warned me against. He said that anything that was said to me, like you are saying, would be because you would be thinking of me as the married woman I was pretending to be."

She saw the expression on the Duke's face and laughed again.

"It sounds rather complicated," she said. "At the same time, as Peter intimated, the compliments you pay me are not for me as I am, but who I am pretending to be."

Now the Duke laughed.

"I can tell you one thing," he said, "I do not think for a moment that you are the quiet and innocent little country-girl you would have me believe. That is the pretence, and you are much more at home as you are now as the bogus Marchioness of Broxburne!"

Carola put her fingers to her lips.

"Do be careful!" she said. "You never know whether somebody might be eavesdropping, and Peter says that Mr. Westwood's man, whom he takes everywhere with him, may be a spy!"

The Duke instinctively looked over his shoulder.

"Does he really think that?" he questioned.

Carola nodded.

"He is a man who has been with Mr. Westwood as his Secretary for many years. It is understood therefore that he should repeat everything he hears to his master."

"Yes—I can see that!" the Duke said slowly. "You are right! We must all be on our guard."

He looked towards the door before he said:

"But just between you and me—what do you think of your 'husband'—now that you have one?"

Because Carola knew he was being curious, the dimples appeared on either side of her mouth.

"Now you are definitely speaking out of turn," she said, "and that is a question I do not intend to answer!"

Before the Duke could say any more she rose to her feet.

"I am a well-behaved, loving, and very faithful wife," she said, "and I can assure you in all sincerity that I have never looked at another man since I married him!"

"Magnificent!" the Duke exclaimed. "But whatever you may do or say, my lovely little Marchioness, I will do my damnedest to make you look at me!"

Before Carola could prevent it, he reached out and took her hand in his.

He raised it to his lips, actually kissing it.

Because she felt embarrassed and a little unsure of herself, she pulled it away quickly.

Without looking back, she walked out of the room.

chapter four

CAROLA thought the dinner was a huge success.

Everybody seemed to be laughing and joking.

She was very conscious that she looked dazzling in the diamond tiara which the Marquis had sent to her by his Valet.

It arrived just as she was putting the finishing touches to her gown.

With it was a diamond necklace and ear-rings to match.

Her finery made her look older.

She thought she was very much "the Marchioness" as she walked down the stairs.

Carola saw the admiration in the Duke's eyes.

She decided not to talk to him, but to concentrate on Alton Westwood.

He was in evening clothes.

But they were obviously cut in the American style.

Mary-Lee looked adorable.

She had on a fluffy dress of the type a young girl would wear.

She was very vivacious, and the men sitting on either side of her at dinner were laughing at everything she said.

With flushed cheeks and shining eyes, no English girl of the same age would have been so self-assured.

At the same time, Mary-Lee was unselfconscious about her appearance.

After dinner they did not go into the Drawing-Room, but into the Music-Room.

To Carola's surprise, a man was at the piano playing the latest dance-tunes.

She looked at the Marquis enquiringly, and he said:

"I understand that both you and Miss Westwood wish to dance, and as there is a shortage of women, I could not spare either of you to be the Pianist."

"You do...you really do wave...a magical wand!" Carola exclaimed.

She was remembering her conversation with Peter in the drive when they arrived.

She saw the Marquis's eyes twinkle at the idea of being a Magician.

"It is a role," he said, "I am quite prepared to assume, but most women tell me I am 'Prince Charming!'"

"I can quite believe that!" Carola remarked. "But Brox Hall is enchanted, and there must be a Merlin about somewhere."

The Marquis laughed.

Then the Duke was at Carola's side to say:

"I think, Marchioness, we should open the Ball together."

There was nothing Carola could do but agree.

The Marquis, as was expected, asked Mary-Lee to dance.

They swung round the room while the other men sat watching them.

Carola was certain they were being very critical.

She noticed, however, that in one corner of the Music-Room there was a card-table.

She was therefore not surprised when the Marquis suggested to Alton Westwood that he might enjoy a game of Bridge.

"I remember," he said, "that you were very fortunate at cards when I was in America."

"If you are looking for your revenge, Marquis, I am quite prepared to accommodate you!" the American replied.

"Because that makes me feel rather nervous," the Marquis replied, "I will make the stakes very low."

Alton Westwood smiled at this.

The Earl and Lord Durrel were obviously eager to make up the four.

This left the Duke to dance with Carola, and Peter partnered Mary-Lee.

The Duke was a very good dancer.

Peter and Mary-Lee were trying out new steps and finding it very amusing.

"Do you need me to tell you how beautiful you look in all your finery?" the Duke asked.

"Compliments make me embarrassed," Carola replied.

"Nonsense!" the Duke exclaimed. "Every

woman enjoys being told she is lovely, especially those who are not!"

"And, of course, it is even more exciting when the compliments are paid by someone as important as a Duke!" Carola said provocatively.

"Now you are laughing at me," he complained, "but actually, my lovely little Pretender, I am completely sincere."

"Do be careful," Carola begged. "You know we all walk a tight-rope!"

"I am enjoying it much more than I expected," the Duke answered.

"If you are indiscreet and mess up the whole thing," Carola said warningly, "the Marquis will never forgive you and neither shall I!"

The Duke raised his eye-brows.

"Does it mean so much to you?"

"It means everything to my brother!"

"Then if you ask me very nicely," the Duke said, "I will obey your command."

The dance came to an end.

Carola sat down on one of the chairs which were on the side of the dance-floor.

"Now let us talk about ourselves," he said.

She did not answer, and after a moment he went on:

"I was just thinking that I would like to see you in the Cumbria tiara. It is one of the largest and most important ever seen outside of Buckingham Palace!"

"Quite frankly," Carola answered, "I would much prefer to wear a wreath of flowers. If I wore even this tiara for long, I would undoubtedly have a headache."

"I wonder what flowers would suit you best!" the Duke mused. "They would have to be something unique and certainly not as commonplace as roses or orchids."

"I am sure you have some very fine greenhouses in your garden!" Carola said conversationally.

She thought she must try to prevent the Duke from being so personal, also from looking at her in a manner which she was afraid would be noticed by the other members of the party.

"You are trying to change the subject," he said reproachfully, "and I think I should warn you, my lovely little Marchioness, that I am a very persistent man."

"I cannot think what you have to be persistent about," Carola remarked.

She looked away from him, watching Mary-Lee and Peter, who once again were dancing.

"Then I will tell you," the Duke said. "From the moment I set eyes on you, I wanted to kiss you, and every moment we have been together since, I am more and more determined that that is what I shall do before the party ends!"

The way he spoke made Carola feel she had to do something about him.

She rose to her feet and, before the Duke could prevent her, walked across the floor to the piano.

"I am enjoying your music so much!" she said to the Pianist. "I wonder if you would play two of my favourite tunes?"

"Of course, M'Lady," the Pianist agreed, "if you will tell me what they are."

Carola mentioned two which she herself played.

They had both been composed by Johann Strauss.

The Pianist smiled.

"I would like to say, M'Lady, they are also two of my favourites!"

He started to play a dreamy Waltz, and as he did so, Carola saw the Duke approaching her.

She deliberately stepped down from the platform on which the piano was placed and walked in the direction of the card-players.

When she reached them, she stood behind the Marquis's chair.

He looked up at her and said:

"Have you come to see if I am losing all our money?"

"I sincerely hope you are not," Carola replied lightly, "and I would like to remind you that I have a birthday next month."

"There you are, Westwood," the Marquis said. "If you take any more out of my pocket, my poor little wife will be very disappointed on the anniversary of her birth."

"It's a date I must remember," Alton Westwood said, "and perhaps the very first automobile that comes off the production-line should be called 'Carola!'"

There was silence until the Earl exclaimed:

"That is an excellent idea, and actually, it is rather a good name for a car."

"It was something I was going to discuss with you," Alton Westwood said. "Perhaps we should have a meeting about it tomorrow."

"That is certainly an idea," the Marquis replied. "In the meantime I want to say 'Two no trumps.'"

The Earl said:

"Three hearts!"

Carola moved away.

She thought, in order to avoid the Duke flirting with her any further, she would sit near the card-players.

There anything he said would be overheard.

He was clever enough to ask Mary-Lee to dance with him, which meant that Peter came towards her.

Because she wanted to talk to him, they went onto the dance-floor.

"Is everything all right?" he asked in a low voice.

"The Duke is behaving in exactly the way you expected he would," Carola answered.

"I guessed that was what was happening," Peter exclaimed, "but all that matters is that Westwood is enjoying himself."

They danced for a few minutes, then Carola said:

"I think, as I am supposed to have been ill, I will now slip up to bed. Will you make my apologies to the others when they have finished their game of Bridge?"

"Of course," Peter agreed, "and you have been marvellous tonight. I am very proud of you."

Carola smiled at him.

"Thank you, Peter, but be careful and do not let anyone drink too much."

Peter nodded.

"I have thought of that '*In vino veritas*' and the last thing anyone wants is the truth at this moment."

Carola gave a little chuckle.

When the music came to an end Peter opened the door for her and she slipped out.

She went upstairs and rang for Jones to come and help her undress.

"Everyone downstairs, M'Lady," the maid said, "was saying how beautiful you looked at dinner!"

"Thank you," Carola answered, "but I am really rather tired and the Doctors have told me I must not do too much too quickly."

"That's good advice, M'Lady," the maid said.

Carola got into bed.

When the maid had left the room Carola picked up the book which she had decided to read.

She was soon enthralled by it.

She had read two chapters and was just thinking perhaps it would be wise to go to sleep.

Suddenly she heard a gentle knock.

It flashed through her mind that it would be Peter come to tell her something.

"Come in!" she called.

To her astonishment, the communicating door opened and the Marquis appeared.

He had obviously undressed and was wearing a long robe.

It was like the one her father had worn and was frogged across the chest, military fashion.

She stared at him as he closed the door and walked towards her.

She thought with horror that something terrible must have happened downstairs.

He had come to tell her about it.

"What...is...it?" she asked. "What has...occurred since...I left?"

He reached the bed and sat down on the side of it without asking if he might do so.

"I had to see you," he said, "and this was my only chance of doing so."

Carola looked at him with worried eyes.

"What is ... wrong?"

"Not exactly wrong," he said, "but I thought I ought to warn you that I must appear to be very affectionate towards you until the party ends."

"Very ... affectionate?" Carola repeated beneath her breath. "Why?"

"I was talking to Westwood this evening," the Marquis explained, "and he told me something he had not mentioned before—that his father was a Lay Preacher."

Carola made a little murmur of surprise as he went on:

"There are a great number of them wandering about America and they are of more importance there than they are here. Westwood was therefore brought up very strictly."

"Y-you mean ... he is ... religious?" Carola asked.

"In his own way—very, and he is certainly extremely shocked at any sort of immorality."

Carola's eyes widened.

"Apparently, when he was coming over in the ship," the Marquis continued, "somebody told him about the *affaires de coeur* of the Prince of Wales and insinuated that everybody who was part of London Society behaved in the same manner."

"And it really ... shocked him?" Carola asked.

"He said he was not having his 'Li'l Gal's' morals corrupted by women who were unfaithful to their husbands, nor, he added firmly, would he allow her to marry a man who was flitting from 'Boudoir to Boudoir' after women who were cuckolding their husbands!"

Carola drew in her breath.

She could understand this was something the Marquis had not expected.

He was watching the expression on her face.

"I can see you understand," he said, "and of course I am extremely nervous that he might not consider me a fit and proper person to be the Chairman of his Company."

"If people gossip, what can . . . you do about . . . it?" Carola asked.

"I took the precaution," the Marquis replied, "just in case Westwood hears any gossip about me, of what I might call 'covering my tracks.'"

"What are . . . you . . . saying?" Carola asked.

She thought it likely that Alton Westwood had already been told that the Marquis was pursuing the beautiful Lady Langley.

Gossip was something no one could prevent.

From all Peter had told her, very little went on in Mayfair without everyone, including the servants, being aware of it.

"What I have told him," the Marquis said, "is that he should not believe everything he hears. There are always people ready to exaggerate and make things sound far worse than they really are."

He gave a dry laugh before he continued:

"That is certainly true, but I think, as I was saying it, that Westwood was sensible enough to guess there is 'no smoke without fire'!"

"But . . . surely," Carola said in a frightened voice, "he would not . . . call everything . . . off that has been . . . planned when it has . . . gone so far?"

"He is quite capable of doing so," the Marquis replied, "and you know what moralists are like— especially Americans, who can be fanatical on any subject that arouses their emotions."

"So . . . what did . . . you say?" Carola asked.

"I told him that because I was so successful on the turf, there were always people ready to be envious of me and who wanted to 'take me down a peg or two.'"

"He understood that?"

"He seemed to, but to make quite certain, I said: 'For instance, I know that people are talking about me because I am constantly with a very beautiful woman; in fact, the most beautiful in the whole of England, whose name is Lilac Langley.'"

The Marquis looked at Carola closely as he spoke.

She knew he was questioning whether she had heard the rumours to this effect.

She tried not to blush, but she felt the colour come into her face.

Despite every resolution, her eyes flickered and she looked away from him.

"Gossip travels on the wind," the Marquis said quickly, "even in the quiet countryside like this."

There was a sarcastic, cynical note in his voice, and Carola said quickly:

"You must not be surprised. After all, you are of great social importance, and my mother always said that the mothers who tried to marry their daughters off to someone with a title could be very bitter when their efforts were thwarted."

The Marquis laughed.

"You are right," he said, "and it is something that does not usually worry me in the slightest, but at this moment I am concerned not with the Dowagers of Mayfair, but with a Puritanical American!"

"What did you say to him?" Carola asked.

"I said he would doubtless hear stories about me and Lilac Langley, but the truth was that I was concerned about her broken heart."

Carola looked surprised and he went on:

"I told him the reason for this was that her husband, whom she adores, is interested in another woman. 'If there is one thing that really upsets me,' I said to Westwood, 'it is seeing a pretty woman in tears!'"

"And he believed you?" Carola asked.

"Of course he did!" the Marquis answered. "My performance was as good as yours!"

"It was certainly a clever explanation," Carola said.

"That is what I thought myself," the Marquis replied, "but you do realise I shall have to be a very attentive husband and convince him there is nothing in the stories he has been told?"

He frowned before he said:

"I only wish I could get my hands on one of these gossipers who cannot keep their tongues to themselves!"

"I am afraid you would be like Canute trying to hold back the tide!" Carola said. "But I realise you must be very certain that Mr. Westwood believes you."

She clasped her hands together before she said:

"It would be too upsetting and too cruel after all the trouble we have taken to open this splendid house if he went back to America or chose another Chairman."

"That is exactly what makes me afraid," the Marquis said, "and perhaps you could see your way clear to telling him what a wonderful husband I am, and how happy we are together."

"Yes, of course I will do that," Carola replied. "Actually I think he is a rather nice man."

"I think so too," the Marquis agreed, "but I did not expect him to have a psalm-singing father who would be more important to him than his snobby desire to have a titled son-in-law!"

"I think Mary-Lee is a very sweet girl," Carola remarked. "But I have the feeling that she has some of her father's obstinacy and intelligence and would not marry merely for a title."

"Do you really believe that?" the Marquis asked. "I thought it was the ambition of every woman to have a 'handle' to their names and if possible to walk in to dinner in front of their mothers!"

Carola laughed.

"Now you are talking about the Dowagers you despise. I am sure all girls, if they are given the chance, want to marry for love, and personally I think arranged marriages are appalling and should be forbidden by law!"

Now the Marquis laughed and he said:

"You are certainly an original young woman, and may I tell you that I am tremendously impressed with the way in which you have taken on a very daunting role which would be hard for a professional actress."

"That is the sort of compliment I want to hear!" Carola smiled. "You must be aware that I have been very, very frightened!"

"I saw the fear in your eyes when I arrived," the Marquis admitted. "I promise I will do everything in my power to prevent you from being upset in any way, and, of course, I am more grateful than I can put into words."

"I am doing this for Peter!" Carola said. "It was very kind of you to ask him to join your important friends."

"I realise that you and your brother are not well off," the Marquis said.

"Things have been very difficult since Papa died," Carola replied, "so it would be wonderful for Peter to have not only a little money, but also something to do."

"That is what I thought myself," the Marquis replied, "and it is the case with all of us of 'Satan finding mischief for idle hands!'"

"Then I will pray very hard," Carola said, "that Mr. Westwood will believe you are the right person to chair his Company, and that your friends are decent, God-fearing men."

She spoke so fervently that the Marquis said quietly:

"I feel sure, Carola, that your prayers will be heard. At the same time, for the next two days we must be very careful."

"Yes, of course," Carola agreed, "and do think of things that will keep all your guests occupied."

The Marquis looked puzzled and she explained:

"If there is a lot of talk it is easy for anyone to make a mistake. Before I came to bed tonight I told Peter to see that no one drank too much."

"That was sensible of you," the Marquis approved, "and something I should have thought of myself."

"Do think of plenty of things for everyone to do tomorrow," Carola said. "Of course there can be riding, and perhaps you can think of something original for them, or somewhere to go in the afternoon."

"I will take your advice," the Marquis said, "and sometime we have to have our Committee meeting."

"And on Sunday . . ." Carola began.

Then she gave a little cry.

"What is it?" the Marquis asked.

"I have just realised that Mr. Westwood will expect everyone to go to Church. It was what I intended to do anyway, but I thought it unlikely that you would do so."

The Marquis thought for a moment.

"I believe in the past my father used to read the Lesson," he said. "That is what I will do on Sunday, and I shall expect my guests to be in the family pew."

Carola gave a little sigh.

"It is just as well you realised that is what Mr. Westwood will expect."

"That *you* realised," the Marquis corrected her, "and thank you once again, Carola, for being so helpful."

He put out his hand as he spoke.

Carola, after a moment's hesitation, put hers into it.

His fingers closed and he said:

"I never imagined when I asked Peter to help me that he would produce anyone quite like you."

"You do not have to be too grateful, because I am also grateful to you," Carola said. "It has been very lonely since Mama died with Peter away in London and nobody to talk to but the old servants."

The Marquis stared at her.

"Are you telling me that you are living alone and without a Chaperone to look after you?"

"There is . . . no one to do . . . that," Carola said quickly, "and we would have to pay a Chaperone. But honestly, I am really quite happy as long as I have a horse to ride and a book to read."

"Then all I can say, looking as you do," the Marquis replied, "that it is the most disgraceful waste of beauty and brains I have ever encountered!"

Carola laughed. Then she said:

"But think how useful they are being to you now. If I had been dancing at every Ball in London, you could not have asked me to come to Brox Hall and . . . pretend to be . . . your wife."

"I certainly would not!" the Marquis said. "But I see your reasoning. At the same time, I feel it is a question that must be considered in the future."

"The . . . future," Carola replied, "for me . . . like you . . . depends entirely on . . . Mr. Westwood."

"Then we both have to do something about it," the Marquis said firmly.

He moved off the bed as he spoke, still holding her hand.

"Thank you again," he said, "thank you more than I can put into words."

His fingers tightened.

She thought for a moment he was going to kiss her hand.

Then before she could realise what was happening, he bent down and kissed her lips.

It was a very gentle kiss, yet because she had never been kissed before, it was a shock.

But it was also strange and exciting.

She had not expected a man's lips to be so hard, and yet at the same time possessive.

It was impossible to breathe.

Then the Marquis raised his head and released her hand.

"Goodnight, Carola!" he said. "Sleep well."

He walked across the room as he spoke, opened the communicating door, and left without looking back.

Only as the door closed and she was alone did Carola give a little gasp.

She had been kissed for the first time in her life and by a man she had met only that afternoon.

It was difficult to realise what she felt and impossible to believe that it had actually happened.

She put out the light and snuggled down in the darkness.

Then she told herself she had asked for an adventure and this was exactly what she was having, a dramatic, unpredictable, amazing adventure such as she had never imagined in her wildest dreams.

How could it be possible that she was in Brox Hall, which she had never entered before?

That she was staying not only with the Marquis, but also pretending to be his wife!

What was more—he had kissed her!

She could still feel his lips on hers.

It gave her a strange feeling within her breast.

She shut her eyes and tried to go to sleep.

Whatever happened the next day and Sunday, when she went back home again she would always have a great deal to remember.

Especially the Marquis—whose lips had touched hers.

chapter five

As Carola came downstairs for breakfast she felt shy.

She was wondering how the Marquis would express the affection about which he had talked to her.

Also, if he remembered he had kissed her.

She told herself firmly it was just an expression of gratitude because she was being helpful.

At the same time, it seemed a very intimate thing.

To think about it made her blush.

She was wearing her riding-habit, ready to challenge Mary-Lee, as they had arranged.

All she had to put on after breakfast was the top-hat that her mother had worn when hunting.

She knew that her habit, although it was old, was well cut.

She had been careful in tying the starched stock round her neck so that it was neat.

However much exertion she expended on horse-back, it would not come undone.

Her father had always said that if there was one thing he really disliked, it was women who had untidy hair when riding.

When she rode with him she had always been particularly careful.

Her red hair was neatly pinned so that not a curl escaped.

She opened the Dining-Room door.

To her relief, the Marquis was not there, nor was the Duke.

The Earl and Lord Durrel were each reading a newspaper as they ate their breakfast.

Alton Westwood was also missing.

The two men rose as she entered and smiled at her.

"Good morning!" they both said, and the Earl added:

"I see you are ready for the fray."

"I am afraid," Carola replied, "considering how much Miss Westwood has ridden on her father's ranch in Texas, I shall be ignominiously beaten!"

The two men sat down again.

She walked to the sideboard to help herself from a long array of dishes.

She thought even an American would be impressed with the varied assortment of food provided for breakfast.

She chose scrambled eggs and sat down at the table.

Her mother had told her what was correct in big houses.

Although there were many servants to wait at other meals, breakfast was always left for the guests to help themselves.

Her father had added that the last thing anybody wanted was for people to chatter early in the morning.

Carola, therefore, did not speak.

She ate her eggs, and spread a piece of toast with Jersey butter which came from one of the Marquis's farms.

She added a spoonful of comb honey which she suspected came from the village.

A great number of the villagers in this part of the country kept bee-hives.

Her mother had always said it was the reason that they were all so healthy.

Carola was just finishing her second piece of toast when the Marquis came into the room with Alton Westwood.

"Good morning, everybody!" he said. "We are late because we have had the most exciting ride, and my American guest, believe it or not, approves of my horses!"

Alton Westwood laughed.

"How could I do anything else?" he asked.

The Marquis walked to the table.

Putting his hand on Carola's shoulder, he bent down and kissed her cheek.

"I hope you slept well, my darling," he said. "I tried to take every precaution so as not to wake you when I went out so early."

"You were successful," Carola managed to say.

His lips against her cheek gave her again a strange feeling.

It was what she had felt in her breast when he kissed her lips.

She also found it difficult to appear at ease.

Having kissed her, the Marquis walked to the sideboard.

"I hope you have left me something to eat," he said, "because I am very hungry."

"So am I!" Alton Westwood agreed.

They discussed the various dishes, which gave Carola time to compose herself.

However, she was aware that the eyes of the other two men at the tables were twinkling.

There was a faint smile on the Earl's lips that she disliked.

The door opened again and the Duke appeared.

"Good morning," he said, "and before you reproach me, I admit I am extremely late as, quite frankly, I overslept."

"The result, no doubt, of our host's good wine, vintage port, and excellent brandy," the Earl joked.

Carola finished her breakfast.

As there was no sign of Mary-Lee, she said to Mr. Westwood as he sat down:

"I hope your daughter has not forgotten that we have challenged each other over the jumps this morning!"

"You can be quite certain that Mary-Lee has not done that!" Alton Westwood replied. "I expect she has had breakfast in her room."

Carola was just about to say she hoped she was not too tired when Alton Westwood explained:

"Mary-Lee has special food for breakfast that she had brought with her from America. I guess she felt embarrassed at eating here and saying she preferred it to what our host has provided."

"Special food?" Carola asked.

"It's some fad that my countrymen have now about people not eating the right food to keep them slim and energetic. Personally, I think it is a lot of balderdash, but American women have gone crackers over it at the moment."

Carola thought this was interesting and was determined to talk about it to Mary-Lee.

She had heard about the enormous meals that the Prince of Wales consumed.

She had read reports in the newspapers of what was provided for guests in smart country houses.

From one newspaper she learnt that besides six or seven courses at luncheon there was an average of ten at dinner.

Also the Prince of Wales enjoyed having a lobster tea.

When His Royal Highness was shooting, a snack consisting of turtle soup and *pâté* was served at midday.

'No wonder he and his friends are fat,' Carola thought to herself. 'If the Americans eat the right food to keep thin, they are very sensible.'

However, the Chef the Marquis had brought down from London had obviously been taught that "Rich and Plenty" must describe every meal.

Now that Carola thought about it, there had certainly been seven courses at dinner last night, not including the dessert.

That had included huge hot-house peaches,

large Muscat grapes, and a varied collection of other fruit.

There had also been Sèvres dishes filled with nuts for the gentlemen to eat with their port.

This might, she thought, be all right for those who were riding all day or taking other sorts of energetic exercise.

But for those who were old or lazy, it must be extremely bad.

She rose from the table saying to Mr. Westwood:

"I will go to see if Mary-Lee is ready."

The Marquis, who had just sat down, said:

"Do that, Dearest, but remember, you are not to do too much, and if you feel tired, we will call the whole thing off at once."

"I will be careful," Carola promised.

He smiled at her.

Then, as he realised she was leaving, he jumped up to open the door.

"As soon as you are ready," he said, "I will be waiting to help you both choose the best horses in the stable."

"Yes, please do that," Carola answered.

She smiled at him.

He put out his arm to pull her for a moment against him.

"You are looking very lovely this morning," he said.

He had lowered his voice as if he were speaking for her ears alone.

Yet Carola was well aware that everybody in the Dining-Room could hear what he was saying.

She slipped away from him and he shut the door.

As she moved quickly along the passage towards

the hall, she was aware that once again she was blushing.

Carola found Mary-Lee dressing and she was astonished at what she was wearing.

It was a divided skirt made in Mexican fashion.

It had a fringe down the side of each leg and round the hem.

The fringes on the jacket matched it.

With it Mary-Lee wore a white blouse with a pattern of green leaves on it.

Carola had seen pictures of this type of riding-gear, but she had never encountered it before.

"My, but don't you look smart and all dressed up!" Mary-Lee exclaimed as Carola stared at her.

"I was thinking the same about you!" Carola laughed.

"Aw—this!" Mary-Lee said. "It's what I wear on Poppa's Ranch and it is more comfortable for jumping than anything you have on."

"I can well believe that!" Carola said. "But you would certainly be a sensation on an English hunting-field!"

Mary-Lee laughed.

"If we come back here in the Winter, I might try it out just to see their faces!"

She had a pretty hat which turned back off her face and fitted comfortably over her hair.

"You make me feel overdressed," Carola complained, "so just to keep you company, I will not wear a hat."

Mary-Lee laughed.

"Then I'll not wear one either! If the men do not like it, they can do the other thing."

She pulled hers off and threw it down on the bed.

The maid helped her into her riding-boots.

They were, Carola noticed, like her own, and sensible for what they were about to do.

Mary-Lee picked up her riding-crop.

"Do you not want some gloves?" Carola asked, conscious that she had the special white string gloves which every woman wore when riding.

"I like the reins between my fingers," Mary-Lee said.

"It is what I like, too, when I am riding alone," Carola conceded. "At the same time, our audience will think it strange."

"Let them!" Mary-Lee retorted. "I am quite certain of one thing—that all the rules and regulations about riding in this country were made by the men!"

"I am sure that is true!" Carola agreed. "And now, if you are ready, let us go downstairs and surprise them."

"Shock them is what you mean!" Mary-Lee laughed. "And it will do them all a lot of good!"

She walked ahead.

As they reached the top of the stairs, Carola saw that the men had come from the Dining-Room and were waiting in the hall.

They were all dressed conventionally.

Perfectly cut white breeches, grey whipcord coats, and riding-boots that shone like mirrors were what they were wearing.

Because she thought that Mary-Lee's defiance was amusing, she deliberately followed her slowly.

Looking over the bannisters, Carola could see the growing astonishment on their escorts' faces.

Only Alton Westwood took his daughter's appearance as being quite ordinary.

Mary-Lee reached the hall.

"Good morning!" she said. "The Marchioness told me you would all be very shocked by my appearance, but I promise you it will not affect my performance."

The men laughed, then the Marquis said:

"You look very attractive, Miss Westwood, as I am sure my horses will tell you."

They walked round to the stables.

The men teased Mary-Lee and looked in surprise at Carola's red hair glinting in the sunshine.

The Duke came to her side.

"Shall I tell you what I think of the way you are dressed?" he asked.

"I know the answer," Carola said coldly, "and I hope you notice how unconventional it is without a hat or gloves."

"Nothing could be lovelier than your hair in the sunshine," he said.

He was speaking in a low voice.

But Carola was afraid Mr. Westwood might overhear him, and she frowned.

"Now you are frightening me!" he protested. "I am much happier when you smile."

She knew he was enjoying teasing her and making her feel nervous.

She therefore walked quickly to the Marquis.

"Have you decided, Alexander," she asked, "which horses Mary-Lee and I are to ride?"

"You have a choice," the Marquis replied, "I

have talked to Peter, and he suggests Red Rufus and Heron."

Carola looked round.

"Where is my cousin?" she asked. "I have not seen him this morning.

"He has been seeing to the jumps," the Marquis explained. "He said some of them wanted strengthening, but he has not had time to attend to them this last week."

Carola knew this was true.

When they reached the stables, Peter was there and the horses they were to ride were already saddled.

"You must choose which one you want," Carola said to Mary-Lee.

"I want something real wild and spirited!" Mary-Lee said. "If I had known this was going to happen, I would have brought one or two of Poppa's horses from the Ranch."

"We will do that another time," Alton Westwood promised.

"Well, come on, then, Poppa, you choose which is the best of these two."

"It is a tough choice," Alton Westwood answered, "and as I have already told our host he has some real fine horses I would not mind owning myself."

Carola thought secretly that they were all for sale if Mr. Westwood was prepared to pay enough for them.

Then the Marquis said:

"I will take that as a compliment, as I am, in fact, very proud of my horses."

There were certainly enough in the stables for everybody.

Carola guessed that the Marquis had brought them from London and Newmarket.

He must have assembled almost every horse he possessed.

There was, however, time to have only a perfunctory glance at those that were in the stalls.

Mary-Lee was obviously eager to go to the paddock.

There were men still working on the fences.

Carola guessed that Peter had been up very early to get everything ready.

She, however, was quite happy when Mary-Lee chose Red Rufus on which to ride and left her with Heron.

He was a large horse and was fidgetting to be off.

This told Carola he had not had enough exercise since he came down from London.

The Marquis mounted a large black stallion which Carola was certain he would not have allowed them to ride.

The other men each chose a horse they fancied which was quickly saddled for them.

They set off, clattering over the cobbled yard.

Then they left by another gate which led onto the flat land.

The paddock was large and the hedges were a good distance from each other.

Carola wondered whether Peter had either raised them or lowered them.

They were certainly quite high, but not in any way dangerous for a well-trained horse.

"Now, the race," the Marquis was saying, "is three times round the paddock and the Winning-Post is where I am standing. The Starting-Post is at the same place, so if you wait for the count of 'three' you can be off."

Carola moved in beside Mary-Lee.

She was thinking as she did so that perhaps Mary-Lee riding astride had a slight advantage over her sitting side-saddle.

At the same time, she could not help thinking that the race would really be for the best horse.

"One—two—three!" the Marquis called.

He had held up his white handkerchief, and as it fell they both started forward.

Carola did not hurry.

Her father had taught her to take things easily at first.

"Hold in your horse," he said, "however hard he wants to compete with a rival."

Mary-Lee therefore took the first fence ahead of her.

She had an expertise which Carola recognised as being exceptional.

There was no doubt that the American girl was a brilliant horsewoman.

Carola knew she would have to ride very hard to hold her own.

At the first time round, Mary-Lee was almost a jump ahead.

At the second, Carola had caught up with her and they were taking the fences almost side by side.

It was as they passed the Marquis for the second

time that Carola saw Mary-Lee was using her crop.

Because her father disliked whips or spurs being used on his horses, she had always managed without either.

Now she settled down to ride in a way she knew he would have appreciated.

The horse she was riding understood.

At the eighth fence she was a little ahead of Mary-Lee.

Then, as the last two loomed ahead, it suddenly struck Carola that it would please Alton Westwood if his daughter won.

It had not occurred to her before that she should be tactful.

Deliberately she pulled in Heron a little before he reached the ninth fence.

It was difficult to hold him.

He knew better than she did that he wanted to beat Red Rufus.

It took all her strength to ensure that Mary-Lee took the last fence a head and shoulders ahead.

She could feel Heron straining as they galloped towards the Marquis.

It was with some difficulty that she managed to prevent him from sweeping past Red Rufus.

A cheer went up from all those who were watching as Mary-Lee passed the Marquis.

"Well done!" "Bravo!" they exclaimed.

Flushed and excited, Mary-Lee pulled in Red Rufus and trotted back.

"I won, Poppa! I won!" she cried to her father.

"You sure did!" Alton Westwood exclaimed.

"And I am real proud of my Li'l Gal. It is one up for the Stars and Stripes."

"Of course it is!" the Marquis agreed. "And we will certainly celebrate this evening. Congratulations, Miss Westwood! You were magnificent!"

He patted Red Rufus, then turned towards Carola.

Heron had just come up alongside him

He patted the horse and said to Carola:

"You are all right, Dearest? It was not too much for you?"

"No, of course not!" Carola replied. "I enjoyed it."

He looked up at her, then in a voice that no one else could hear he said:

"Thank you! That was very tactful."

Carola looked down into his eyes.

She was glad he understood.

He realised she could, if she had wanted to, have won the challenge.

Then the Duke, who was on the other side of her, complimented her on her riding.

The Marquis turned away.

It was the men's turn to jump the fences.

When they had done that to their satisfaction, they all galloped over some of the Marquis's flat land.

After that they rode home through the woods.

"What you want on your fields, Marquis," Alton Westwood was saying, "is some of the new machinery I am using on my Ranch in Texas. It does the work in half the time, and I am sure these fields, with the right treatment, could produce first-class crops."

101

"I am sure they could," the Marquis answered, "but I am sure the machinery you are talking about would cost a great deal of money. That is why my Estate is neglected."

"Then it's something, Marquis, we will have to alter in the future," Alton Westwood remarked.

He spoke so positively that Carola, who was listening, thought the Chairmanship was the Marquis's.

Unless, of course, something unforseen happened to prevent it.

'I am so glad for him . . . so very, very . . . glad!' she thought.

*   *   *

When the party got back it was luncheontime.

Carola and Mary-Lee changed their riding-clothes for elegant, pretty gowns.

"What are we doing this afternoon?" Mary-Lee asked.

"I am sure my husband has something very exciting planned for us," Carola answered. "He is so enjoying having your father here."

"I am enjoying it too," Mary-Lee said, "and I am glad I won the jumps."

"Another time I shall wear sensible clothes like you had on," Carola said, "then perhaps I will have a better chance."

Mary-Lee laughed.

"That would shock the men more than they have been already. I could see they were looking down their noses at me and thought I was just an

102

ignorant American who does not know how to behave."

"I am sure they were thinking nothing of the sort," Carola said.

"Of course they were," Mary-Lee insisted, "and if you want the truth, I have a habit something like yours which I wear in New York, but I thought it was good for the English to see that the American view can be different from their own."

Carola laughed.

She thought Mary-Lee was a great deal more intelligent than most people might have expected her to be.

It was very brave of her to deliberately dress unconventionally.

As Carola went to her own room she could not help thinking that the Marquis was foolhardy in not considering Mary-Lee as his wife.

He needed money so badly to keep up his magnificent house and estate.

Mary-Lee was not only lovely, but also clever enough to adjust herself to a grand position.

At luncheon she certainly kept the men on either side of her laughing.

When the meal was over, the Marquis had arranged that they should drive over to see a Folly.

One of his ancestors had built it about two miles away from the house.

"It has a marvellous view over four Counties," he said, "and I want Mr. Westwood to be impressed by it."

"What is depressing me," Westwood remarked, "is that you keep calling me 'Mr!' My name is Alton to all my friends, and if we are not friends by this time, then all I can say is that we ought to be!"

"You are quite right," the Marquis agreed, "and I am delighted to call you Alton. As you know, my name is Alexander."

The other men said the same thing, giving him their Christian names.

Listening, Carola thought with amusement that this was very un-English.

She knew that the gentlemen usually either addressed each other by their surnames, or, in the case of the Duke, the Marquis, and the Earl, by their titles.

'We will all become Americans before we are finished!' she thought.

She felt that the Marquis's ancestors in their gilt frames were looking down on them with disapproval.

She and Mary-Lee went upstairs to put on their hats.

Carola also found a parasol which she had brought with her in case they sat about in the sun.

Her mother had always been very firm that she was not to spoil her white skin by getting sunburnt.

She was aware, however, that because Mary-Lee had lived on a Ranch in America and rode without a hat, she had a golden tinge to her clear skin.

It was very becoming to her, but then, her hair was not red.

As they went downstairs there was a variety of vehicles outside.

The Marquis and Peter had taken them out of the store. They had been there for generations.

There was a High-Perch Phaeton which had been the fashion in the reign of George IV and an early Chaise which had been built at the beginning of Queen Victoria's reign.

There was also an open Britchka Chariot which had been invented by Count d'Orsay, the lover of Lady Besborough.

There was a great deal of amusement at their appearance.

The Marquis insisted upon driving the Phaeton and taking with him Carola and Peter.

"I am not leaving my wife to the mercy of any of you!" he told the other men. "And, Duke, I suggest you take Alton in the Britchka Chariot which requires very careful driving. I think Mary-Lee will be safer in the Chaise."

Mary-Lee was quite content to sit beside the Earl.

At the last moment, Lord Durrel said he had never been in a Phaeton and was longing to ride in one.

He therefore changed places with Peter.

They set off, and Carola was thankful that the Marquis drove so well.

"I have often wondered," she said, "how they managed the High-Perch Phaetons on the very bad roads they had then, but I remember reading that the Prince Regent held the record to Brighton in five hours and twenty minutes."

"I could easily beat that today with my horses and on better roads!" the Marquis remarked.

"One day you had better try it," Lord Durrel said, "I am sure somebody at Whites Club would be prepared to wager you a large sum that they will beat you in a donkey-cart or something equally unlikely."

The Marquis laughed.

Carola thought that when the weekend was over she would always remember what fun it was, so very different from what she had expected.

Alton Westwood was duly impressed with the Folly.

They all drove home to a large, if late, tea.

Carola ate very little because she did not want to spoil her appetite for dinner.

When they went upstairs Mary-Lee entered her bedroom first.

Then, just as she was going towards her own, which was at the end of the corridor, Carola heard Peter calling her.

She stopped, and as he reached her he said in a low voice:

"I must speak to you."

She was about to say he could come into her bedroom, when she remembered that the maid was there.

Peter knew what she was thinking.

He opened the door of a room opposite which was not being used by any of the guests.

As he shut the door behind him Carola asked in a worried voice:

"What is . . . it?"

"I have just realised," Peter said, "that although Alton wants to go to Church tomorrow, and the Marquis had arranged for us all to accompany him, you cannot go with us!"

"Why not?" Carola asked.

Then before Peter could reply, she knew the answer.

"You think there might be somebody..." she began.

"...who would recognise you!" Peter finished. "Of course they might. After all, other people in the County go to Church, and they would certainly be astonished to learn that the Marquis was married and they had never heard anything about it."

"Oh...of course!" Carola exclaimed. "Oh, Peter, what a good thing you thought of it!"

Then she gave a little sigh.

"All the same, I would like to go to Church on Sunday," she said. "You know I always do."

"You can always say your prayers," Peter remarked, "and Heaven knows, we all need them, in the Chapel."

"In the Chapel?" Carola exclaimed. "I had no idea there was one."

"Naturally there is," Peter said as if she were being very stupid in not being aware of it. "The trouble is, I have had so much to do that I have not had time to put it in order."

"I will certainly go there to say my prayers anyway," Carola said. "Where is it?"

"It is quite easy for you to find," Peter said. "You pass the Marquis's door, and at the end of this passage you will find a staircase which is not often used."

Carola was listening intently as her brother went on:

"It leads directly to the Chapel, which was convenient for the Master of Brox Hall in the old days.

I imagine they were a good deal more religious than they are today!"

"I will find it," Carola said. "But just in case Mr. Westwood wants to look at it, you had better ask the gardeners to bring in some flowers, otherwise he may criticise the Marquis for having neglected it."

"Yes, of course," Peter said, "that is a good idea. And by the way, Carola, everyone is stunned by the brilliant manner in which you are carrying this off."

"We still have quite a long way to go," Carola said in warning, "so we must be really very careful."

"That is what I am trying to be," Peter replied.

Dinner was an amusing meal and wholly delicious.

Afterwards, instead of going to the Music-Room as Carola expected, the Marquis took them to the Billiard-Room.

This was in another Wing.

It was a huge room containing an enormous Billiard-Table which was very skilfully lit.

There were also several different games that Carola had not expected to find there.

There was a small Skittle-Alley, a Dartboard, and an amusing game of Hockey.

This could be played by four people manipulating the ball with sticks which had to be turned at the side of the table.

Carola played this with the Earl.

Then the Duke insisted that she have a game of Skittles with him.

After a few mistakes at first, she became quite skilful.

She was enjoying the game until, realising the rest of the party were engaged, the Duke said in a low voice:

"I want to talk to you alone. You must know that you are driving me crazy!"

"Do be ... careful!" Carola murmured. "You know you are in deep ... mourning for ... your wife!"

"I am tired of this farce!" the Duke complained in a petulant tone. "It is quite warm. Come and walk with me in the garden."

"You know quite well that Mr. Westwood would be very ... shocked!" Carola replied.

"Damn Alton!" the Duke exclaimed. "I am fed up with watching Alexander mooning over you and you knowing it means nothing. I want to tell you what I feel about you, Carola, which is a very different thing."

"I think it is ... time I went ... to bed," Carola said. "Goodnight ... Your Grace!"

She moved away from the Skittles and went up to the Marquis.

He was playing Billiards with Mr. Westwood.

"I am a little tired," she said, "and I know you will understand if I go to bed."

"Of course I understand, and I think it very sensible of you, darling," the Marquis replied. "I will see you to the stairs."

He put down his cue and said to Mr. Westwood:

"Forgive me a moment, Alton. My wife is slipping off to bed, and as I do not want to disturb her when I go up, I will say goodnight to her now."

He did not wait for the American to reply.

He put his arm round Carola's waist and drew her to the door.

When they were outside he set her free.

"You have been marvellous!" he said. "And someday I will be able to say so more ardently."

"There is still tomorrow," Carola warned.

"I have not forgotten," the Marquis replied.

They reached the bottom of the stairs.

Carola noticed there was a footman on duty in the hall.

However, the Marquis was aware of him too, and he merely lifted her hand and kissed it.

She felt his lips touch her skin before she started up the stairs.

"I will not be late coming to bed," he said. "We have had a long day."

"And a very enjoyable one," Carola said from the top of the stairs.

She hurried to her room and rang for Jones to come and undo her gown.

It was a relief to be able to get into bed.

At the same time, she still wanted to read a little.

She opened her book.

Then she knew that after the hard ride this morning and the drive this afternoon, she was tired.

She shut her eyes, expecting to fall asleep.

Instead, she found herself thinking about the Marquis.

She was still feeling his lips on her hand.

She wondered if he was missing Lilac Langley

and longing for the time when he could return to London and see her again.

She heard the footsteps of people coming up to bed and the sound of doors being shut.

She was still awake.

She thought she was, in fact, rather thirsty.

She got out of bed and pulled back the curtains slightly.

The moonlight streamed in, and there was no need for any more light to guide her to the wash-handstand.

On it there was a jug of water for her to drink.

She stood for a moment entranced by the beauty of the night. The moon and the stars seemed to fill the sky.

It was so lovely, so part of her dreams, that she felt it could not be real.

She stood transfixed, oblivious for the moment of everything but the enchantment that dazzled her eyes.

Suddenly she heard a sound behind her.

Carola turned her head.

She was aware that the door leading out into the corridor was being opened very slowly.

For a moment she could hardly believe it.

Then she felt that it must be Peter, who had come to tell her that something had gone wrong.

The door opened a little farther.

Now a man was silhouetted against the light of the sconces outside in the corridor.

Her heart seemed to stop beating.

She knew who it was and was suddenly des-perately afraid.

There was no mistaking his height and his square shoulders.

As he came farther into the room she was aware of the communicating door near where she was standing.

Swiftly and silently in her bare feet she reached it.

Turning the handle, she managed to slip into the next room.

chapter six

THE Marquis's room was in darkness and Carola stood as if looking into a void.

Her whole body was shaking.

Before she could think of what she should do, a door opened on the other side of the room.

The Marquis came in.

He was carrying in his hand a candelabrum with four lighted candles.

He set it down on a bedside table, and as he did so Carola ran towards him.

She flung herself against him.

As his arms went round her she said in a whisper that was almost incoherent:

"The . . . the . . . D-Duke has . . . come to my . . . r-room and . . . I am . . . f-frightened!"

The Marquis could feel her trembling against him, and for a moment he just held her.

Then he said in a low voice:

"I will deal with this."

He sat her down on the bed.

Then he walked across the room until he reached the communicating door.

Carola had not shut it behind her. She had only pushed it to.

The Marquis realised there was a gap that would bring a streak of light into the room.

In his ordinary voice he said aloud:

"As I was telling you, Peter, you and Carola must be very careful what you say in front of Alton Westwood. He told me again this evening how shocked he was at what he had heard of the behaviour of London Society."

He paused, then, as if Peter or Carola had replied to what he said, he laughed.

"That of course is true," he said. "At the same time we cannot expect people from other countries to understand all the peculiarities of our own. But I remember my father always used to say that we are an insular people, especially where it concerns our pleasures."

As he finished speaking he listened and was sure he heard the sound of a door closing.

He went back across the room to Carola.

She was sitting on the side of the bed, where he had left her.

Her eyes seemed to fill her face because she was so afraid.

She seemed oblivious to the fact that she was wearing a thin, transparent nightgown.

Her red hair fell over her shoulders almost to her waist.

She looked so lovely that the Marquis could understand the Duke's desire to be alone with her.

He was, however, very angry about it.

He sat down beside her.

"It is all right," he said in a quiet voice. "He has left now."

Carola gave a little cry and turned her face against his shoulder.

"I...I never thought...never imagined...he would...come to my bedroom," she murmured.

"I expect he wanted to talk to you," the Marquis said. "It is difficult to do so when there are so many people listening."

"He s-said," Carola went on, "that he...wanted to...kiss me...but...I do not want...him to."

The Marquis thought that the Duke would want a great deal more than a kiss.

He realised that Carola was so innocent that she would not understand, and he said:

"I am quite sure he will not come back."

He felt a little tremour go through Carola's body before she said:

"It was...clever of you to...pretend that... Peter was...here."

"Actually," the Marquis said as he smiled, "I am rather proud of myself, but it would be a mistake to accuse the Duke of being overfamiliar."

"I have been...trying to...avoid that...I have...really!" Carola said pleadingly.

She did not want the Marquis to think she had encouraged the Duke, that she had flirted with him so that he thought he could take liberties with her.

"I noticed that," the Marquis replied, "and I thought it was very sensible of you to come to me for help. At the same time, Carola, he is a Duke and unmarried."

Carola raised her head.

He could see the astonishment in her eyes.

"Y-you do not...mean...?" she began.

She paused and went on:

"But...he is...old...very old...and it never...crossed my mind that he might be...in l-love with me."

"You are very beautiful," the Marquis said quietly, "and you have to get used, Carola, to men losing their hearts when they look at you, whether they are old or young."

Carola shivered before she said:

"I think the...sooner I can...go back to...living quietly with only...my horses for company...the better!"

The Marquis smiled.

"I think that would be a great waste of your looks and, of course, your brains, which we have talked about before."

"I never...imagined that...anyone like...the Duke would...come to my room! Mama... would be...horrified!"

"I think she would also be shocked at you pretending to be my wife," the Marquis said, "but you are aware that by doing so you have now saved me and, of course, Peter from being continually in need of money."

Carola gave a little gasp of excitement.

Then she exclaimed:

"You mean...everything is settled? You are to be the Chairman and Peter is on the Board of Directors?"

"It was all arranged this evening before dinner," the Marquis said, "and unless something terrible happens, it will be signed and sealed as soon as we get back to London."

"I am glad... so very... very... glad!"

"And I am very grateful," the Marquis said.

Carola got to her feet.

"Do you think it is safe now for me to go back to my room?" she asked a little nervously.

"Yes, I am sure it is," the Marquis replied, "but let me first make certain."

He rose, walked across the room, and opened the communicating door.

With the moonlight shining through the window he could see that Carola's room was empty.

The door into the corridor was closed.

He felt Carola move up behind him.

"Has he... really... gone?" she whispered.

"You can see for yourself," the Marquis answered, "but so that you will not worry, I will lock your door while you get into bed."

When he had done so he turned round.

In the moonlight she looked ethereal and insubstantial, like a Princess in a Fairy Tale.

The Marquis stood looking at her without speaking.

She pushed back her long hair from her shoulders before she said:

"Thank you... thank you for... being so... kind and... understanding. Perhaps it was... stupid of me to be... so frightened... but..."

"What you did was very sensible," the Marquis assured her. "You came to me, and if there are any more disturbances in the night, whether they be ghosties, ghoulies, or human beings, remember—I am next door."

117

Carola laughed at the way he spoke, as he meant her to do.

Just as she thought he was about to leave her she put out her hand.

"You may think me . . . very foolish," she said a little hesitatingly, "but . . . could you leave the door between us . . . open? Then if I do . . . scream you . . . will hear . . . me."

"I promise you I am a very light sleeper," the Marquis answered. "If you should call me, I will come at once."

"Thank . . . you."

The Marquis took her hand in his.

"Now go to sleep," he said. "I want you to look especially lovely tomorrow so that Alton goes back to America thinking that whatever else Society may be like, our Marchionesses are very beautiful."

Again Carola laughed and answered:

"I am sure, whatever . . . you may . . . say, he will . . . find an American woman who will . . . eclipse the English."

"I expect you are right," the Marquis agreed. "At the same time, when I do marry, it will *not* be to an American!"

He spoke so firmly that Carola was surprised.

Instead of kissing her hand, he put it gently down on the sheet in front of her.

"Goodnight, Carola," he said, and his voice was very deep.

"Goodnight," she answered. "Once again . . . you have waved . . . your magic . . . wand and . . . everything is . . . enchanted!"

118

"That is what I want it to be," the Marquis said quietly.

He walked to the window and closed the curtains, shutting out the moonlight and the stars.

Then he went from the room, leaving the communicating door open behind him.

*   *   *

The Marquis had given his Valet Dawkins instructions to call him early.

He intended to ride before breakfast.

He had invited Alton Westwood to ride with him, suggesting they should have some exercise before it was time to go to Church.

The American said it was something he would greatly enjoy.

The Marquis promised to take him to a part of the Estate where they had not been before.

"There are some hedges there," he said, "too high for any woman to jump, but I think you will enjoy them."

"I sure will!" Alton Westwood replied.

The Marquis was helped into his clothes by his Valet in silence.

He disliked talking first thing in the morning.

When he was ready, Dawkins, who had been with him for many years, said:

"I thought I ought to let Your Lordship know, that yesterday, when one of th' new servants was down in th' village, he says they was a-talking about some nasty-lookin' strangers who was asking if you, M'Lord, 'ad an American staying 'ere."

"Strangers?" the Marquis enquired sharply.

119

"They was a-sayin' in th' shop as they talked in a strange manner through their noses an' I were a-wonderin', M'Lord, if that meant trouble for Mr. Westwood."

The Marquis was frowning.

"It certainly seems odd that there should be Americans in our village," he remarked, "but it would be better to say nothing to Mr. Westwood, or his man-servant."

"That's what I thinks, M'Lord, but in case there be any trouble, I've got Yer Lordship's revolvers here with us."

"Where have you put them?" the Marquis asked.

"In th' chest-of-drawers, M'Lord, th' old one and the new one you buys afore we went across th' Atlantic."

"Then let us hope we do not need them," the Marquis said. "At the same time, Dawkins, keep your eyes open. I know nothing happens of which you are not aware!"

"Leave it to me, M'Lord!" Dawkins grinned.

The Marquis left his bedroom and went downstairs.

Stevens the Butler was waiting for him.

The horses that he and Alton Westwood were to ride were outside.

"How many Nightwatchmen are on duty?" the Marquis asked.

"Two, M'Lord," Stevens answered. "I believe Sir Peter appoints them before we came down from London."

The Marquis nodded.

At that moment Alton Westwood came hurrying down the stairs.

*   *   *

Carola had ordered her breakfast in bed.

She had to excuse herself from going to Church because she had a headache.

The Marquis had, she told Jones, insisted on her taking things easy.

She guessed he would inform Alton Westwood that she had done too much yesterday with the riding and driving, besides, of course, seeing to the comfort of their guests.

"My wife never spares herself," he said.

"I've noticed that," Alton Westwood replied, "and I think you're a very lucky man!"

"I assure you I am well aware of it!" the Marquis had replied.

Carola looked at the sunshine outside her windows.

She could not help wishing that she could go riding before breakfast.

The Marquis's horses were so superb.

She knew when she reached home she was going to find Kingfisher and the other horses in their stables very slow.

'It is disloyal of me,' she thought, 'but I would like to ride Heron again before I leave.'

She had, however, an interesting book and read it while she ate her breakfast.

It was nearly an hour later before there was any need for her to get up.

Jones came to help her and she was nearly dressed when the maid said:

"Miss Westwood didn't go to Church with the gentlemen, M'Lady."

Carola was surprised.

"She is still in the house?"

"Yes, M'Lady. His Lordship drove off about half-an-hour ago, but Miss Westwood was still asleep and she's only just woken up."

Carola thought Mary-Lee must have gone to bed very late last night.

She arranged her hair.

It took much longer than when she did it in her usual manner.

There was a knock on the door, and Mary-Lee came into the room.

"I was told you had not gone to Church," she said, "and I was asleep when they left, so I expect Poppa will be annoyed at my missing Services on Sunday."

"I had a headache," Carola replied, "but it is gone now, so I am going down to the Chapel. Perhaps you would like to come with me?"

"There is a Chapel—here?" Mary-Lee asked. "How exciting! I would like that."

"You will find that most 'Stately Homes,' as they call these big houses in England, have their own private Chapels," Carola explained.

"I call that a real smart idea!" Mary-Lee said. "And when I tell Poppa about it, I guess he'll want one back home!"

Carola laughed.

"Then we must certainly show him the Chapel when he returns."

She rose from the stool in front of the dressing-table as she spoke and said to Jones:

"Thank you so much. Will you leave out the hat that goes with this gown? It has white camellias on it. I expect we will go driving after luncheon."

"Very good, M'Lady, and if you wants me, just ring th' bell," Jones replied.

"I will do that," Carola answered.

Mary-Lee was waiting, and she slipped her arm through Carola's as they left the room.

"There is a staircase at the end of the corridor," Carola said, remembering what Peter had told her. "It leads down to the Chapel. It was convenient in the old days when the Marquis of Broxburne of the time wanted to say his prayers."

"You've got to tell all that to Poppa," Mary-Lee said. "He is convinced that compared to us Americans the English are all heathen in their ways!"

"Then we must enlighten him," Carola said. "And I am delighted to hear that he has not yet a private Chapel of his own!"

"I am sure he will have one as soon as he gets back," Mary-Lee predicted.

They walked to the end of the corridor.

There was the staircase, as Peter had told her.

It was very different from the grand one they habitually used with its crystal chandeliers and a gilt balustrade.

There was, in fact, only room for them to move down it side by side.

Then there was a passage before they came to the door of the Chapel.

It was small but must originally have been beautiful.

Carola could see there were a lot of repairs which needed doing.

Several of the stained glass windows were cracked or broken.

But Peter had not forgotten to tell the gardeners to bring in some flowers.

There were two vases of them on the altar and on either side of it huge pots of Madonna lilies which had just come into bloom.

There were also flowers on the window-sills, and Carola thought the whole place looked very attractive.

It was arranged in a strange manner with carved pews which must have been placed there when the Chapel was first built.

They were set down the sides of the Chapel so that the centre aisle was left clear.

It seemed strange until she thought, when a Marquis or a member of the family died, they would lie in State.

There was room for a large coffin in the centre aisle.

Now there were two *Pries-Dieu* in front of the altar with satin cushions on which to kneel.

The two young women went instinctively towards them and knelt down.

Carola began to pray silently that everything would continue as well as it was at the moment, also that, as the Marquis had told her, the contracts involving them all would be signed in London.

Then she was suddenly aware that there were men behind her.

* * *

Upstairs, Dawkins was just coming out of the Marquis's bedroom when Jones emerged from Carola's.

"Oh, there you are, Mr. Dawkins!" she exclaimed. "Do you know where Her Ladyship's gone?"

"She's gone to th' Chapel," Dawkins replied, "an' Miss Westwood's gone with 'er."

"You wouldn't believe it," Jones said, "but I clean forgot to give Her Ladyship a handkerchief. I put it down on the bed and found it just now when I was tidying up."

She hesitated a moment before she said:

"Do me a good turn, Mr. Dawkins, and nip down and give it to Her Ladyship. I don't like to be neglectful in my duties!"

She held out the handkerchief as she spoke, and Dawkins took it from her.

"If I do this for you," he said, "what are you goin' to give me for me trouble? I'd settle for a kiss!"

"Go on with you!" Jones replied. "I'm too old for that sort of nonsense, and so are you, if it comes to that!"

"That's where you're wrong!" Dawkins replied. "There's life in the old dog yet, as I'll prove if you'll give me half a chance!"

Miss Jones turned away with a little flounce of her skirts.

125

"You'll be lucky!" she said.

Dawkins chuckled, and, holding the handkerchief, went down the stairs in the direction of the Chapel.

He was walking along the passage when he saw the door ahead was open.

Outside, to his surprise, he could see a carriage.

He knew that something was happening in the Chapel.

It suddenly occurred to him that something was wrong.

Why should there be people entering Brox Hall without coming to the front-door?

Being thoroughly familiar with the house, he knew there was a door beside him which led into the Vestry.

He went through it to where there was a curtain over the entrance to the Chancel.

It took him only a second to reach it.

He peeped through the side of the curtain to see what was happening.

To his horror, he realised that two men were at that very moment putting heavy sacks over the heads of Carola and Mary-Lee.

The two young women were kneeling at the *Pries-Dieu*.

The men moved swiftly so that their cries were stifled by the sacks.

The men pulled them down to the women's waists.

They then tied a rope round them to make sure they could not be pulled off.

Dawkins saw their arms were close to their sides.

The rope prevented them from moving any part of their bodies except their legs.

It all happened so quickly.

The next second the men had lifted the young women up and carried them over their shoulders out of the Chapel.

They then threw them into the carriage that was waiting outside.

Dawkins had not been with the Marquis for so long without being almost as quick-brained as his Master.

He left the Vestry and ran up the stairs into the Marquis's bedroom.

He took the two pistols from the drawer and put them into his pocket.

Then he ran downstairs again.

This time he went in the opposite direction from the Chapel and towards the stables.

One of the things the Marquis did every year was to go with the County Yeomanry of which he was a member, on its manoeuvres.

He always took Dawkins with him.

The two horses which he used as Chargers were used to gunfire.

When Dawkins reached the stables he gave his orders and those two horses were saddled at record speed.

Dawkins mounted one.

Leading the other by the bridle, he rode towards the Church as quickly as he could.

The Church was situated inside the Park close to the entrance to the Drive.

As he reached it, the Service had just ended.

Two village boys were hanging about outside,

and Dawkins told them to hold the horses for him.

Hurrying to the Church, he saw the Marquis being escorted down the aisle by the Vicar.

He was leaving before anybody else, and the rest of his guests were walking behind him.

As they reached the main door the Marquis was saying:

"Goodbye, Vicar, and thank you for a delightful Service. It is a pleasure to be home again."

"It is a great joy to have you here, My Lord," the Vicar replied, "and everybody has been greatly cheered by the sight of Brox Hall being opened and Your Lordship in residence."

"Thank you," the Marquis replied.

He was walking towards his carriage, aware that a footman had already opened the door, when he saw Dawkins.

"What is it, Dawkins?" he asked.

Dawkins stood on tip-toe so that he could reach the Marquis's ear.

"The young American lady and Her Ladyship 'ave bin kidnapped, M'Lord!" he whispered. "I thinks I knows where they've gone. I've brought Your Lordship two Chargers an' the revolvers."

Just for a moment the Marquis was still.

Then he said quietly:

"Thank you, Dawkins," and beckoned to Peter.

As Peter came towards him the Marquis said to the Duke:

"Take Alton back to the Hall, will you? I have just learnt that one of my farms is on fire and Peter and I will go to see what we can do about it."

"That is bad luck and I . . ." the Duke began.

128

The Marquis, however, was not listening.

He was already hurrying towards the horses.

As he reached them Dawkins pushed one of the revolvers into the pocket of his coat.

Then the Marquis sprang into the saddle.

Dawkins hurried to Sir Peter and gave him the other pistol.

He covered it with his free hand so that the boy holding the horse could not see what was happening.

The Marquis paused long enough to say:

"Where do you think they have gone, Dawkins, and how many of them?"

"Four, M'Lord, and, judging by the carriage which 'as two 'orses, I reckons they're makin' for London."

"That is what I expected," the Marquis agreed.

He urged his horse forward as he spoke.

Only as they were riding at a quick trot through the village did Peter ask:

"What has happened? I realise it is serious!"

"Kidnappers!" the Marquis replied. "I was warned this morning, but paid no heed, and if anything happens to Mary-Lee or Carola, it will be my fault!"

"You mean—they have carried them off?" Peter asked in disbelief.

"In a carriage with two horses," the Marquis replied, "and we have to stop them before they reach the main road. They will not be able to go very fast in these narrow lanes."

As he finished speaking he spurred his horse forward and Peter did the same.

The lanes were, in fact, narrow, twisting and with huge hedges on either side.

Peter thought it would be impossible for a carriage of any sort to move quickly however many horses were drawing it.

At the same time, he realised that the Marquis was tense and he was also extremely worried.

He knew that nothing could upset Alton Westwood more than to have his adored daughter kidnapped.

Even if they were fortunate enough to rescue the two girls, it might make the American cancel all his plans.

He would return to his own country.

The Marquis was riding very fast.

It was only because Peter was riding a horse equally well-bred that he was able to keep up with him.

They had travelled for nearly two miles.

The Marquis was aware that the road to London was just ahead.

Then, as they turned a sharp corner of the lane, they saw a carriage ahead of them.

And the Marquis gave a deep sigh of relief.

Peter drew as near to him as he could.

"What are we going to do?" he asked.

"There is a ford about a hundred yards farther on," the Marquis replied. "The horses will have to slow down considerably, and it is then we will go into action—and it must be simultaneously."

The Marquis told Peter exactly what they would do.

They galloped on, and were aware that the carriage in front of them was slowing down.

130

The ford could be deep and dangerous in the Winter.

Yet, because there had been very little rain in the past month, it was only about a foot deep in the middle.

At the same time, the two horses pulling the carriage had to cross it at a walk.

It was just as the first one had stepped into the water that the Marquis and Peter acted.

The sun was high in the heavens and it was very hot.

As the Marquis had anticipated, the windows of the carriage were lowered.

Also, he could see that the two young women, bound and covered, were on the back seat.

There were two men sitting opposite them with their backs to the horses and two men on the box.

The Marquis and Peter fired simultaneously, hitting the outside arms of the men inside the carriage.

They screamed as they were hit.

A second later the Marquis and Peter fired again, this time at the driver and the man sitting beside him on the box.

Again they hit their arms and the wounded men yelled in agony.

The horses reared and, if they had not been harnessed to the carriage and in the Ford, they would have bolted.

But that was impossible, so they merely neighed and reared.

The Marquis and Peter dismounted.

Opening the doors of the carriage, they pulled

out the two men inside it by the backs of their collars.

The man the Marquis hauled out was clutching at his injured arm.

But, as he was thrown on the ground, he made an attempt to pull out his revolver.

The Marquis was too quick.

He took it from him and threw it into the water of the Ford.

He turned back to the carriage to lift out Carola.

Peter, on the other side of the carriage, was lifting out Mary-Lee.

The men on the box, in agony at having been shot, had fallen to the ground.

The one that was nearest to Peter had dropped his revolver which he must have been holding in his hand.

As Peter lifted Mary-Lee from the carriage he kicked the weapon into the Ford.

Then he started to untie the rope from around her waist.

He pulled the sack off her head.

Half-stifled and very afraid, when she saw his face she flung her arms round his neck.

"Y-you...saved...me!" she murmured, and burst into tears.

The Marquis had undone the rope and pulled the sack off Carola.

She had known as soon as she heard the shots that in some miraculous way he had come to save them.

She had, in fact, been very frightened as she was being carried from the Chapel.

The man holding her had thrown her roughly down onto the seat of the carriage.

As she felt Mary-Lee joining her she knew what was happening.

She wondered frantically how it would be possible for the Marquis to find out what had occurred.

The men had not spoken.

But as the carriage had started off she was aware of their feet touching hers.

She knew that there must be two of them and that they were sitting on the opposite seat.

She realised she and Mary-Lee were in a terrifying situation.

There had been nobody else in or near the Chapel.

It was clever of the men to have spirited them away at a time when the Marquis and his house guests were all at Church.

The kidnappers must have known, she thought, where they would be.

Carola suspected they had bribed one of the hired servants.

They must also have been waiting for just such an opportunity when Mary-Lee would be alone and defenceless.

She was of no consequence, but they could not leave her to tell what had happened.

The carriage rumbled on, moving at a fast pace through the village.

Carola had longed to cry out for help from the people they must be passing.

She thought no one would notice a particular carriage driving away from the Hall.

133

She expected it would be a very long time before the Marquis at Church had any idea of what had occurred.

Then, very much sooner than she had expected, the shots rang out.

She heard men screaming in pain.

She had known then that they were saved.

Now, as she looked into the Marquis's eyes, she saw the relief in them.

In a voice that did not sound like her own she said:

"Y-you came ... how could ... you have been ... so clever to know ... where we ... were?"

The Marquis did not answer.

He merely picked her up in his arms and put her on the saddle of his horse.

As Dawkins had been well aware, the two Chargers were unperturbed by the shooting.

They had started slightly when the shots first rang out.

Then, when their riders dismounted, they grazed by the roadside.

The Marquis looked at Peter on the other side of the carriage and saw that he was kissing Mary-Lee.

They were completely oblivious to the groans of the men and the foul language that accompanied them.

"Let us get out of this mess!" the Marquis said.

Peter raised his head.

He did not answer.

He merely saw that the Marquis had lifted Carola onto his saddle.

Picking up Mary-Lee, he did the same.

Then the Marquis and Peter swung up behind the two young women.

As they turned their back on the wounded men and the still-floundering horses, Peter said:

"I congratulate you, Alexander, and if we ever have to go to war, I am quite prepared to serve under you!"

"You were... both wonderful... wonderful!" Mary-Lee cried.

She spoke in a choked little voice because the tears were still running down her cheeks.

Peter tightened his left arm round her.

Both men rode their horses slowly back along the lane in the direction of Brox Hall.

When they had gone some way, the Marquis was aware, because he was holding her so close to him, that Carola was not as frightened as she had been.

"I hope, Mary-Lee," he said, "your father is not going to be extremely upset about this!"

"Does Poppa know what has happened?" Mary-Lee asked.

The Marquis shook his head.

"No. Thanks to Dawkins, who brought the horses to the Church, nobody else knows. I told our party that Peter and I were attending to a fire at one of the farms."

Mary-Lee gave a little cry.

"Please do... not tell... Poppa!" she begged. "You must... not tell... him!"

"Must not tell him?" the Marquis repeated in surprise.

"Of course not!" Mary-Lee insisted. "He will only get into a terrible fluster. When this happened once before in America, I had a simply awful time."

She paused, gave a sob, then continued:

"I was surrounded by guards day and night. I could hardly take a bath without them peeping in to see that I was still there!"

She drew in her breath before she said:

"Please . . . please . . . do not tell Poppa! It will spoil . . . everything!"

Carola was aware that the Marquis had suddenly relaxed.

The tension she had felt when he was holding her to him seemed to vanish.

"If you really mean that," he said to Mary-Lee, "then this must be a secret which none of us must divulge to anybody."

"That would be . . . marvellous!" Mary-Lee exclaimed. "I could just not bear all the fuss that happened last time when Poppa wanted to go out and shoot the kidnappers!"

"Then I promise you that no one will know what has just occurred," the Marquis said, "and when we get nearer to the house, you and Carola must just walk in as if you had been admiring the garden."

"We will do that," Mary-Lee said, "but I am so . . . very glad that you were . . . clever enough . . . to come and . . . save us."

"I . . . too am . . . glad," Carola murmured.

She looked up at the Marquis as she spoke and thought how marvellous he had been. What of her kidnappers? All that was over now . . .

She was aware as she did so that her face was very near to his.

She could not help thinking it would be very wonderful if he kissed her again, just as an expression of delight because she was no longer a prisoner of those wicked men.

He did not reply to what she had said.

He was looking ahead at the lane down which they were proceeding.

Then so suddenly she felt her heart turn over, she knew that she loved him.

She felt her whole being vibrate to his.

What had been a pretence had, as far as she was concerned, suddenly become a reality.

There was no pretence about what she felt. It was love.

The love she had wanted and prayed for—the love which was Divine.

The world seemed transfigured because he was in it.

But she knew how hopeless her love was.

He loved someone else and was as out of reach as the Moon.

chapter seven

As they neared the house the Marquis said:

"I will put you down somewhere near here."

Carola gave a little cry.

"We must go in by a side door," she said. "I am sure I look terrible after being covered with that disgusting sack!"

The Marquis looked at her hair curling over her forehead, a great wave of it falling over one shoulder.

"You look very lovely!" he said.

For a moment she felt her heart contract at the depth in his voice and what she thought was the expression in his eyes.

Then she told herself that, as Mary-Lee could hear what he said, he was only play-acting.

She turned her face away and did not look at him again until he stopped at the back of the garden.

"Go in by the garden door," he said. "No one will see you until you reach your rooms."

"That is very sensible," Mary-Lee said.

Peter, having dismounted, lifted Mary-Lee gently from the saddle.

Carola thought he held her close in his arms for longer than was necessary.

Then she told herself they had all been through a very traumatic experience and all he was doing was soothing Mary-Lee, who seemed still to be upset.

They walked in through a gate which led them behind the yew-hedges and into the main part of the garden.

As they went, Carola heard the horses being ridden away and knew they would go to the stables.

Only as they went up a side-staircase to the First Floor did she wonder what was the time.

So much had happened that, if anyone had told her it was late in the afternoon, she would have believed them.

Instead of which, to her surprise, when she entered her bedroom and looked at the clock on the mantelpiece, she saw it was only five minutes to one.

Jones was waiting, and she gave an exclamation of horror when she saw her mistress's hair.

"What have you been doing to yourself, M'Lady?" she asked.

"I got caught up in a thorn bush," Carola said quickly. "It was stupid of me, but I am sure you will not take long in making it look tidy again."

"Of course I won't, M'Lady," Jones replied, "but you'd best be careful. I caught my finger on one and it took a long time healing."

Carola did not answer.

Now that she was back she felt suddenly limp because the tension was over.

She thought she would never forget how frightened she had been when, blinded and unable to move, she had felt the carriage moving away and thought no one would ever be able to find them.

She knew the kidnappers had not been after her, but Mary-Lee, because she was rich.

At the same time, that might mean they would treat her roughly or perhaps dispose of her in some way.

She told herself, however, there was no point in going on thinking about it.

The Marquis, in his usual brilliant way, had saved them, and she was quite certain he would take care that sort of thing never happened again.

They must be very grateful to Mary-Lee for deciding that her father should not be told.

It would be a tragedy if Mr. Westwood should return to America determined to "wash his hands" of the English.

"Have a look at yourself, M'Lady," Jones was saying.

Carola glanced in the mirror and thought it extraordinary that there were not deep lines on her face, or that her hair had not turned white after what she had been through.

Instead, she looked just as usual, and she hoped the Marquis would really think, as he had said, that she was lovely.

'Do not be so foolish!' she admonished herself. 'And if he is in love with the most beautiful woman in England, why should he pay any attention to you, unless it is to his advantage to do so?'

She went downstairs, and as she reached the hall she could hear voices in the Drawing-Room and knew that the Marquis and Peter had joined the others.

She went in to find them, as she expected, enjoying a drink before luncheon.

"Ah, there you are, my dearest!" the Marquis exclaimed, walking towards her. "I was beginning to wonder what had happened to you!"

He put his arms round her and kissed her cheek and, although she tried hard not to be thrilled by it, she felt a little quiver run through her whole body.

"It was so lovely in the garden that I lost all track of time!" she explained.

The Marquis put a glass of champagne into her hand.

"I think you deserve this," he said.

He had his back to the others and they could not hear what he said.

"You were very clever," Carola answered.

Mary-Lee came bursting into the room.

"If I am late, you are not to be angry with me!" she said, speaking to everybody. "But the Marchioness and I had such a wonderful time all amongst the flowers!"

She walked up to her father, kissed him, and said:

"I am sorry I did not go to Church with you, Poppa, but I just overslept."

"You missed a fine Sermon," Alton Westwood said.

Luncheon was announced, and they all went into the Dining-Room.

It was an amusing meal.

At the same time, Carola could not help feeling a little limp, and she knew it was the reaction after all that had occurred in the morning.

As they were leaving the Dining-Room the Marquis said as they walked down the corridor:

"I think you ought to rest, darling. You must have walked quite a long way this morning, and you know what the Doctors said."

"Y-yes...of course," Carola replied. "I do feel a little tired."

"Try to sleep," he said, "and if you do not feel like coming down for tea, I am sure Miss Westwood will play hostess on your behalf."

"Of course I will!" Mary-Lee said. "But Peter and I are going to see the horses. I hear you went to the stables after you had been to Church."

"That is right," Alton Westwood said, "and I can tell you, I was very impressed. But unfortunately our host was taken away to deal with a fire."

"It was a false alarm," the Marquis said loftily, "or, rather, a very small one, and I would much rather have been with you."

"And what are you planning for us this afternoon?" Alton Westwood asked.

There was a short pause before the Marquis replied:

"I thought, as it is sunny, you would rather spend a more restful afternoon than we have been doing on the other days. I have, in fact, quite a lot of correspondence to deal with."

"I tell you what we will do," Alton Westwood said. "We will have another meeting immediately after tea which will save time when we are back in London."

"That is a good idea," the Marquis approved. "I am sure you have a lot of things to do and I have already told my Secretary to arrange for my private coach to be attached to the Express train which will stop at the Halt at nine-thirty."

He paused a moment before he went on:

"That means we will be in London in just over an hour, and have everything signed and sealed before luncheon."

"That certainly suits me," Alton Westwood agreed.

All the men approved of this and, Carola thought, the Marquis was making sure that the party was over and he could go back to living his own life without worrying about the affairs of Brox Hall.

She went upstairs and, without ringing for Jones, took off her shoes and put her feet up on the bed.

She did not pull the curtains because she liked to see the sunshine coming through the windows.

She was, in fact, more tired than she had thought herself to be, and very soon she fell asleep.

* * *

Carola awoke with a start and realised she had been dreaming about the Marquis.

It seemed very real. She was disappointed to find

143

it was only a dream and she was still on her bed and alone.

She looked at the clock.

She was horrified to find that it was five o'clock, and she must have missed tea.

'I will go down at once!' she thought, putting on her shoes.

She hurried down the stairs and entered the Drawing-Room to find all the men there with the exception of Peter. Mary-Lee was also missing.

"I am so sorry to be late," she said. "I do hope you have not waited tea."

"We were indeed waiting for you, darling," the Marquis said as he smiled, "and Miss Westwood was not here to take your place."

"I do apologise," Carola said. "My only excuse is that I fell asleep."

"That is just what I wanted you to do," the Marquis replied. "I thought you were looking pale before luncheon, but now, darling, the roses are back in your cheeks!"

"That is very poetical." Carola laughed.

"He is telling the truth," Alton Westwood said, "and I could not have expressed it better myself."

Carola smiled at him and started to pour the tea.

There were, as usual, many delicious things to eat, but she did not feel hungry.

She was only acutely conscious of the Marquis, thinking how handsome he looked and feeling that her heart was behaving in a strange way every time he spoke to her or came near to her.

"I love him!" she told herself unhappily. "But after tomorrow I shall never see him again!"

Because she hoped against hope that Alton Westwood would stay a little longer in England, she asked:

"When are you and Mary-Lee returning home to America?"

"On Tuesday," he answered, "just as soon as everything is completed here with your husband in charge. I have to get back to the factory and see what is happening to my automobiles."

"I am sure they will be everything you hope for," Carola said.

"I shall be very disappointed if they are not!" Alton Westwood replied.

"And so shall we all!" the Marquis exclaimed, who had been listening to the conversation.

As he spoke, the door opened and Mary-Lee came in accompanied by Peter.

"Where have you two been?" Alton Westwood asked.

Mary-Lee ran to her father.

She put her arms round his neck and, looking at him, she said:

"Oh, Poppa, I am so happy! I have never been so happy in my whole life!"

Alton Westwood looked at her in surprise and Peter, who was just behind her, said:

"And I am feeling exactly the same, Sir. I think you will guess that Mary-Lee has done me the great honour of promising to become my wife!"

Alton Westwood stared at Peter in astonishment, and the Marquis exclaimed:

"Well done! That is the best news I have heard in a long time! Congratulations, Peter!"

He held out his hand as he spoke, and the other

men clustered round to do the same thing.

"So, you have decided to marry this young Englishman!" Alton Westwood said at length to Mary-Lee.

"I love him, Poppa, and he loves me," Mary-Lee said simply.

The Marquis noticed the expression in Alton Westwood's eyes and thought it was one of disappointment.

Quickly he went up to the American and put his hand on his shoulder.

"I think, Alton, I should congratulate you," he said, "on having as your future son-in-law a young man who represents one of the oldest families in English history!"

The American looked at him questioningly and the Marquis went on:

"The Gretons came over with William the Conqueror, and ever since they have distinguished themselves in one way or another."

He stopped speaking to smile at Westwood before he continued:

"A Greton was knighted at the Battle of Agincourt. Another was a Statesman at the Court of King Henry VIII, and Peter is the Sixth Baronet after the title was created by James II."

He laughed before he added:

"His Family Tree is longer than mine, and it is something which always annoyed my father!"

"I had no idea of this!" the American said, but now he was smiling and the Marquis knew there would now be no opposition to the marriage.

Carola kissed Peter.

"I hope you will both be very happy, dearest," she said.

"We will be!" Peter said positively.

The men were clustering round Mary-Lee, making their congratulations and excuses to kiss her cheek.

She was laughing and enjoying the excitement of it and Peter drew Carola to the window.

"We will make plans later," he said, "and I will discuss with the Marquis how we will eventually tell Westwood that you are my sister."

"Whatever you do," Carola warned, "wait until after tomorrow, when everything has been settled."

"I am not a fool!" Peter replied.

He paused, then he said:

"I love Mary-Lee, Carola, and I would marry her if she had not a penny to her name. She wants to live in England and she is longing to see Greton House."

"Then she will not be going back to America on Tuesday?" Carola asked.

Peter gave a short laugh.

"I have not had time to think of anything for the moment except telling Mary-Lee that I love her. We will sort out everything else when we are alone, and after I have talked it over with Alexander."

"Yes, of course," Carola agreed.

Peter went back to Mary-Lee's side as if he could not bear to be apart from her.

The Marquis sent for champagne so that they could all toast the future Bride and Bridegroom.

Carola was also aware that he was enlightening

Alton Westwood with more facts of the Greton family.

She was surprised he should know so much.

She then thought it was typical of his efficiency that he would know the background of everybody who was to be involved with him and the company of which he was now the Chairman.

She was suddenly aware that the Duke was trying to get close to her.

Therefore, having drunk to Mary-Lee and Peter's healths, she ran upstairs to her room.

There was just time for her to rest a little more before dinner.

*   *   *

Carola put on one of her prettiest gowns and added for the last time some of the beautiful jewellery the Marquis had brought down from London.

Her gown was very pale blue, the colour of the sky in Spring.

She had found among the jewels a turquoise necklace, ear-rings, and bracelets.

They were all set with diamonds, but there was nothing to wear on her hair.

She had a sudden idea.

She sent a message to the gardeners through the footman who was bringing round a tray of flowers for the Gentlemen to choose for their buttonholes.

It took a little time, but just before Carola was to go downstairs for dinner a wreath arrived that was made of white orchids with a sprinkling of forget-me-nots between the blossoms.

It looked so lovely and so elegant that Carola felt no jewelled tiara could equal it.

She saw the admiration in the Duke's eyes the minute she entered the Drawing-Room.

She was not certain, however, from the way the Marquis looked at her, whether it was with admiration or just appreciation that she was playing her part so well.

At dinner everybody seemed to be in particularly good form, teasing the future Bride and Bridegroom, who were seated side by side, both looking radiantly happy.

"One thing is quite certain," the Marquis remarked. "If you go on your honeymoon in one of your father's motor cars, it will receive a tremendous amount of publicity and sell a large number to other prospective Brides and Bridegrooms!"

Mary-Lee gave a little cry of protest.

"We have no intention of waiting until the automobiles arrive in England!" she said. "And if you want to attend the wedding, you will have to come to America next month!"

"So soon?" the Duke exclaimed in surprise. "What has our Chairman to say about that?"

The Marquis merely made an expressive gesture with his hands.

"When two people are in love," he said, "time stands still!"

"We are being married in New York," Mary-Lee announced, "and Poppa is going to give us the biggest wedding and, before it takes place, the largest Ball that New York has ever seen!"

The men laughed and throughout the meal offered suggestions and new ideas not only for the honeymoon but also for the ceremony.

When Carola and Mary-Lee went into the Drawing-Room, Carola put her arms around her and said:

"I am so happy for you and Peter!"

"He is the most wonderful man I have ever met," Mary-Lee said, "and I assure you we are going to be very, very happy!"

"Of course you are!" Carola agreed.

"He told me," Mary-Lee went on, "that he had no intention of marrying anyone, least of all an American, but as soon as he saw me he knew I was the girl he had been waiting for, and he is not going to risk losing me!"

"I have known Peter for many years," Carola said quietly, "and I have never seen him in love before, as he is with you."

"I will look after him," Mary-Lee said, "and once we are married we are going to live in England in the house that means so much to him."

"That will be lovely for you both," Carola said.

As she heard the men coming towards the Drawing-Room, she said to Mary-Lee:

"Tell them I have gone to bed."

As she spoke she slipped out of the room through one of the long windows which opened into the garden.

She hurried across the lawn until she was out of sight of the house, then went more slowly.

The moonlight turned the garden to silver and the sky was bright with stars.

It was so beautiful that it seemed to Carola wrong that instead of lifting her heart as it had last night before the Duke had come into her room, as far as she was concerned the whole world was dark.

She was thinking that first, because Peter would take Mary-Lee after their marriage to Greton House, where she herself had been very happy, there would be no place for her.

Secondly, and this was frightening, there was the question of how Alton Westwood was to be told she was not Peter's cousin, but his sister.

Lastly, sooner or later, he would have to learn that the Marquis was not married.

All these problems seemed to raise their heads like ogres threatening the future for the Marquis and Peter.

At first she was too frightened to even begin to think of a solution.

Then, as if the answer came to her through someone outside herself, she knew that the only thing she could do which would ensure everybody's happiness but her own was to disappear.

The Marquis could inform Alton Westwood, once he was back in America, that she had died.

That way there would be no reproaches and no recriminations.

"That is what I have to do," she told herself, "and the only question is—how soon?"

She had at least a little time left, because Mary-Lee was first going back to America, and Peter was going with her.

It would merely be a question of the Marquis and the rest of the Board going over there with him.

Reasoning it out, she thought it would be best if she "died" before they went so that there would be no uncomfortable questions as to whether the Marquis was married or not.

Anyway, the business could be put in hand long before they went, in fact as soon as they reached London the next day.

'I must try and think where I can hide myself,' Carola thought frantically.

It would be best, she thought, if she left the country altogether.

She tried to think of one of her friends who lived in France or in any other part of Europe.

She walked on a little farther to where, behind some bushes that were in blossom, there was a wooden seat where she could sit down.

She had a view of the top of the house with the moonlight shining on the statues on the roof.

There was the Marquis's standard flying high above them like a sentinel.

She thought when she had to go away tomorrow it would be a sight she would never see again.

She knew she could not bear to ride past it as she had done before, knowing she could no longer enter through the front-door.

She could no longer hear the Marquis talking to her in his caressing voice, and no longer be aware of him as he stood beside her.

"I love him! I love him!" she whispered, and felt the tears begin to roll down her cheeks.

She shut her eyes at the pain of it.

Suddenly a voice beside her said:

"Not crying, Carola?"

He must have come to her side over the lawn.

She gave a little start and put her fingers up to her eyes.

The Marquis sat down beside her, and taking a handkerchief from his pocket, wiped her cheeks, then her eyes.

"There is nothing to cry about," he said gently.

"B-but . . . there is!" she answered through her tears. "I have been thinking about the . . . tangle we are in . . . and I know the only . . . thing I can d-do is to . . . disappear!"

"Disappear!" the Marquis asked.

"You can . . . s-say I had died," Carola said a little incoherently. "It would be . . . best for me to have . . . d-died before the . . . wedding."

The words seemed to choke in her throat.

Once again the tears filled her eyes.

Because she was angry with herself for being so unrestrained, she took the handkerchief out of the Marquis's hand and wiped her eyes roughly.

"You really think I should say you are dead?" he asked very quietly.

"There is . . . nothing else you can do," Carola said, "and . . . sooner or later . . . you will have to tell Mr. Westwood that . . . P-Peter is my . . . brother and not my cousin . . . which was one lie . . . and I am sure he must . . . never . . . never know that we were not really m-married . . . he would be terribly shocked."

"I am aware of that," the Marquis said.

"S-so you . . . do see it is the only . . . solution to everything that I should . . . disappear and you become a . . . widower?"

There was silence for a moment. Then the Marquis asked:

"Is that what you want?"

It was such an absurd question that Carola

longed to tell him it was the last thing in the world she wanted.

To be exiled from everything that was familiar, and most of all from him, would be an unbelievable hell.

Instead, she said briefly:

"It is the ... only thing we can do."

"And you planned all this without consulting me!" he said.

"I was ... thinking of you," she answered, "and you will have the Chairmanship without any trouble.

"It matters to you and ... it matters to your friends ... and of course it matters to Peter."

"You are very unselfish and very sweet," the Marquis said, "but also very foolish."

"I ... I do not know why you should say that," Carola stammered.

"Do you really think I would let you sacrifice your whole life just because I wanted money and the position whereby I can make it?" the Marquis asked.

"I ... I will be ... all right," Carola said.

"But I will not!" the Marquis answered. "At the same time, it is very wonderful of you to think of me, and I am deeply touched, Carola."

"Then ... you will do as I suggest?" Carola asked.

"I will most certainly not!" the Marquis answered.

Carola stiffened.

"But you must ... you must understand ..."

"I do understand," he said, "and you have answered the one question which I was going to ask

154

you when we had the chance to be alone."

"The . . . question?"

"It is quite simple," the Marquis answered. "I need to know, Carola, what you feel about me, not as somebody who is helping Peter and, of course, myself—but as a man!"

Carola stared at him.

She thought in the moonlight he was looking very handsome.

It made her heart beat very much faster because he was there.

His arm was lying across the back of the seat behind her.

Then as she tried to think of an answer to his question she said a little hesitatingly:

"I . . . admire you . . . I think you are very . . . clever and . . . of course . . . you have a solution to everything . . . but there is no other solution except mine . . . to this problem."

"That is where you are wrong!" the Marquis contradicted her. "My solution is far better than yours. As I have said, you have already given me the answer to the question I would have put to you."

Carola did not understand, and she looked at him enquiringly.

"I think," the Marquis said slowly, "if you are honest and truthful, you will admit that you love me a little."

Carola started.

It was not what she had expected him to say, and she felt her cheeks burn as she turned her head away from him.

She could think of nothing more humiliating

than for him to think that she loved him and be sorry for her because he loved somebody else.

"It is important for me to know the truth, my precious," the Marquis said, "because, although I have been afraid of frightening you by telling you, I love you very much!"

For a moment the whole world turned upside-down and Carola thought she could not have heard him aright.

Then, as she tried to ask him what he was saying, thinking it could not be true, his arms went round her.

He pulled her against him, then even before her lips parted to speak, his mouth held her captive.

He kissed her gently, yet at the same time possessively.

She felt she must be dreaming.

It was what she had longed for ever since the first time he had kissed her.

Now his kiss was very different, and she knew that he took her heart from her body and made it his.

Now her love welled up within her, seeping through her body with an inexpressible ecstasy into her breast and then to her lips.

It was a wonder beyond anything she could imagine, and as the Marquis drew her closer and still closer she thought if she died now she would have known the wonder and perfection of Heaven whilst still on Earth.

Only when he raised his head did she manage to say incoherently:

"I . . . love you . . . of course I love you . . . but I never thought that . . . you could . . . love me!"

"I have loved you since the first moment I saw you," the Marquis said. "I could not believe anyone could be so lovely. But, my darling, I was so afraid of frightening you, as Cumbria did."

"I was ... never frightened of you ... once I knew you," Carola whispered.

"I will never let you be frightened by anyone again!" the Marquis promised.

His lips were on hers, and he kissed her until Carola was sure they were both flying in the sky and the stars had moved into her breast.

Only when they were both breathless did the Marquis say, as she put her head on his shoulder:

"My sweet, my darling, is there anyone more perfect? How can you make me feel like this?"

"Y-you ... do love me ... really love me?" Carola asked. "But ... I thought you ... l-loved ..."

He put his fingers over her lips.

"I have never loved anybody but you," he said. "There have been women in my life—of course there have—with whom I was infatuated and who delighted me because they were beautiful. But what I feel for you, my sweetheart, is completely different."

"How ... different?" Carola asked.

"It will take me a long time to tell you how different," he answered, "but it will be easier after tomorrow night."

"Tomorrow night?" she asked in a puzzled tone.

"We are being married very quietly and secretly, here in the Chapel, as soon as I return from London."

Carola felt she could not be hearing aright.

"M-married?" she murmured.

"I told you that my solution was a better one than yours," the Marquis said as he smiled, "and I have planned it all out."

Carola gave a choked little laugh.

"I might have guessed you would!"

"You should have trusted me," he said, "and, in fact, it is something I have been planning ever since I knew that I could never lose you. And however long it took, I would eventually make you my wife."

"I want . . . to be your wife . . . I want it desperately!" Carola said. "But . . . are you sure that I am the . . . right person for you? Also . . . how can we be married without Mr. Westwood being . . . aware of it?"

"I have told you to trust me," the Marquis said. "I have arranged with the Vicar, who is also my Private Chaplain, that we will be married at about six o'clock tomorrow evening. Nobody except Dawkins will have the slightest idea what is taking place, and he will be on guard to prevent anybody from interfering with or kidnapping us!"

"Please make sure they do not do that!" Carola begged.

"I will make sure of everything," the Marquis assured her, "and I have already thought of an explanation for pretending to Westwood that you were Peter's cousin rather than telling him you were really his sister."

"What is that?" Carola enquired.

"I shall say—after everything is signed and sealed, of course—that I did not wish him to think I was pushing my relatives upon him when I suggested that Peter should join the Board of the Company."

Carola made a little murmur but did not interrupt as the Marquis went on:

"I am sure Westwood will accept it at its face value, and also he will be delighted that Mary-Lee is more closely linked with my family, as you will be her sister-in-law."

Carola laughed.

"I am sure he will. You think of everything!"

"Ever since we first met I have been unable to think of anything but you!" the Marquis said. "And what I will not have is you worried, upset, or frightened!"

"I love you!" Carola murmured.

"I want to hear you say that over and over again," the Marquis said, "and it is what I know you will say when we are on our honeymoon."

"Can we really . . . have a honeymoon?" Carola asked.

"I have every intention of having one," he said, "and after we are married tomorrow, while Stevens, who wants to stay with me, arranges some permanent staff for the house, you and I are going to my Hunting Lodge in Leicestershire."

He paused a moment to smile at her before he continued:

"We shall have few neighbours to disturb us at this time of the year, my precious, and I will have you alone to tell you how much you mean to me, how much I love you, and how you are more beautiful than any woman I have ever seen!"

"Do you . . . mean that? Do you . . . really mean it?" Carola asked eagerly.

She was thinking of the beautiful Lady Langley and being afraid she would compare with her unfavourably.

"I swear to you on my life, which I hold sacred," the Marquis said, "that you are more beautiful than any woman I have ever seen and I want, as I have never wanted anything in my life, to own you, to possess you, and to be certain you are mine alone."

Carola came a little closer to him.

"That is . . . what I want," she whispered.

"It is what you will be," he answered, "and, darling, there are a great many things we will be able to do together. Most important, we will start by improving the house and the Estate so that it will be as it was in my grandfather's time, and make the people who live on it happy and prosperous."

"I want to do that," Carola said a little breathlessly.

"There are many other things for us to do, not only in the Social World, but also in the Political World, where I know we can help a great many causes which I will now be able to do more efficiently in Parliament, and I will be able to afford not only time, but also money to alleviate distress and neglect."

"I would love to help you in that. You are so wonderful . . . so clever!" Carola cried.

"And you must not forget that I am magical," the Marquis said, "and, darling, it is a magic which we will give to everyone who comes near us. It is the magic of love—the love I have dreamt of and longed one day to find but thought impossible."

"Now . . . I can give it to you," Carola murmured.

The Marquis did not answer in words.

He kissed her until they were both trembling with the wonder and ecstasy of it.

The moonlight enveloped them and the stars seemed to twinkle excitedly in the sky.

As the Marquis held Carola closer and closer, she knew they were no longer two people but one.

One indivisibly joined together, from now until Eternity.

Barbara Cartland, the world's most famous romantic novelist, who is also an historian, playwright, lecturer, political speaker and television personality, has now written over 537 books and sold over 500 million copies all over the world.

She has also had many historical works published and has written four autobiographies as well as the biographies of her mother and that of her brother, Ronald Cartland, who was the first Member of Parliament to be killed in the last war. This book has a preface by Sir Winston Churchill and has just been republished with an introduction by Sir Arthur Bryant.

Love at the Helm, a novel written with the help and inspiration of the late Earl Mountbatten of Burma, Great Uncle of His Royal Highness The Prince of Wales, is being sold for the Mountbatten Memorial Trust.

She has broken the world record for the last sixteen years by writing an average of twenty-three books a year. In the *Guinness Book of Records* she is listed as the world's top-selling author.

Miss Cartland in 1978 sang an Album of Love Songs with the Royal Philharmonic Orchestra.

In private life Barbara Cartland, who is a Dame of the Order of St. John of Jerusalem, Chairman of the St. John Council in Hertfordshire and Deputy President of the St. John Ambulance Brigade, has fought for better conditions and salaries for Midwives and Nurses.

She championed the cause for the Elderly in 1956 invoking a Government Enquiry into the "Housing Conditions of Old People."

In 1962 she had the Law of England changed so that Local Authorities had to provide camps for their own Gypsies. This has meant that since then thousands and thousands of Gypsy children have been able to go to School, which they had never been able to do in the past, as their caravans were moved every twenty-four hours by the Police.

There are now fourteen camps in Hertfordshire and Barbara Cartland has her own Romany Gypsy Camp called Barbaraville by the Gypsies.

Her designs "Decorating with Love" were sold all over the U.S.A. and the National Home Fashions League made her, in 1981, "Woman of Achievement."

She is unique in that she was one and two in the Dalton list of Best Sellers, and one week had four books in the top twenty.

Barbara Cartland's book *Getting Older, Growing Younger* has been published in Great Britain and the U.S.A. and her fifth cookery book, *The Romance of Food*, is now being used by the House of Commons.

In 1984 she received at Kennedy Airport America's Bishop Wright Air Industry Award for her contribution to the development of aviation. In 1931 she and two R.A.F. Officers thought of, and carried, the first aeroplane-towed glider airmail.

During the War she was Chief Lady Welfare Officer in Bedfordshire looking after 20,000 Service men and women. She thought of having a pool of Wedding Dresses at the War Office so a Service Bride could hire a gown for the day.

She bought 1,000 gowns without coupons for the A.T.S., the W.A.A.F.'s and the W.R.E.N.S. In 1945 Barbara Cartland received the Certificate of Merit from Eastern Command.

In 1964 Barbara Cartland founded the National Association for Health of which she is the President, as a front for all the Health Stores and for any product made as alternative medicine.

This is now a £650,000 turnover a year, with one third going in export.

In January 1988 she received *La Médaille de Vermeil de la Ville de Paris*. This is the highest award to be given in France by the City of Paris for achievement—25 million books sold in France.

In March 1988 Barbara Cartland was asked by the Indian Government to open their Health Resort outside Delhi. This is almost the largest Health Resort in the world.

Barbara Cartland was received with great enthusiasm by her fans, who fêted her at a reception in the City, and she received the gift of an embossed plate from the Government.

Barbara Cartland was made a Dame of the Order of the British Empire in the 1991 New Year's Honours List by her Majesty the Queen for her contribution to literature and also for her years of work for the community.